The Pendragon's Challenge

The Last Pendragon Saga:
The Last Pendragon
The Pendragon's Blade
Song of the Pendragon
The Pendragon's Quest
The Pendragon's Champions
Rise of the Pendragon
The Pendragon's Challenge

The Lion of Wales series:
Cold My Heart
The Oaken Door
Of Men and Dragons
A Long Cloud
Frost Against the Hilt

The Gareth and Gwen Medieval Mysteries:
The Bard's Daughter
The Good Knight
The Uninvited Guest
The Fourth Horseman
The Fallen Princess
The Unlikely Spy
The Lost Brother
The Renegade Merchant
The Unexpected Ally

The After Cilmeri Series:
Daughter of Time (prequel)
Footsteps in Time (Book One)
Winds of Time
Prince of Time (Book Two)
Crossroads in Time (Book Three)
Children of Time (Book Four)
Exiles in Time
Castaways in Time
Ashes of Time
Warden of Time
Guardians of Time
Masters of Time

Book Seven in *The Last Pendragon Saga*

The PENDRAGON'S CHALLENGE

by

SARAH WOODBURY

The Pendragon's Challege
Copyright © 2016 by Sarah Woodbury

This is a work of fiction.
All rights reserved. No part of this publication may be reproduced, stored in a retrieval system, or transmitted in any form or by any means without the prior written permission of the author, nor be otherwise circulated in any form of binding or cover other than that in which it is published.

*To Taran,
who's really liking these books*

A Quick Recap of the Last Pendragon Saga ...

Last we saw Cade, Rhiann, and their friends, they had defeated the armies of Mercia, led by Cade's uncle, King Penda, at Caer Fawr, a hillfort in eastern Wales. Penda, along with his son Peada (who had once intended to marry Rhiann), had been seduced by Mabon, the son of Arianrhod and Arawn, the Lord of the Underworld. Much of the damage sustained in that battle had been *glamour* arranged by Mabon. Once he returns to the Otherworld and Penda's folly is revealed, Penda asks Cade to ally with him in Mercia's own fight against another Saxon lord, Oswin of Northumbria.

Cade refuses to join his uncle, in large part because the battle had revealed to Taliesin and Cade the real danger they faced: the Thirteen Treasures of Britain were in play, and more *sidhe* than just Mabon and Arianrhod were meddling in the human world. They decide that in the months before Cade's crowning as High King of the Britons, set for the day of the summer solstice, Cade must return to Dinas Bran to consolidate his rule over the Kingdom of Gwynedd. Taliesin, meanwhile, would set out immediately in search of the rest of the Treasures.

The Pendragon's Challenge picks up the story three months after the events of *Rise of the Pendragon*.

Cast of Characters

Cadwaladr (Cade) ap Cadwallon—King of Gwynedd
Rhiann ferch Cadfael—Cade's wife (Queen of Gwynedd)
Cadfael—Rhiann's father, King of Gwynedd (deceased)
Cadwallon—Cade's father, King of Gwynedd (deceased)
Alcfrith—Cade's mother
Penda—King of Mercia
Peada—Penda's son
Oswin—King of Northumbria

Beli—King of the Otherworld
Arianrhod—Goddess, Beli's daughter
Arawn—Lord of the Underworld
Mabon—Arianrhod's and Arawn's son
Gwydion—Arianrhod's brother

Cade's Companions

Taliesin—seer/bard
Goronwy—knight
Catrin—seeress
Dafydd—knight, Goronwy's brother
Angharad—Dafydd's wife
Bedwyr—knight
Hywel—knight

1

Dinas Bran

June 655 AD

"We ride!" The shout echoed all the way to the top of the keep. "Hail Cadwaladr! King of the Cymry! The king shines forth!"

The gate opened, and the host of cavalry surged forward. The narrow causeway between the ramparts was full of Mercians, but the riders swept down the pathway, their arms swinging, taking out every enemy within reach, even as they picked up speed. All the way down from the fort, the hapless Mercians fell under the horses' hooves or—those who were less lucky—to one side, where a sword sliced through them.

Then they reached the field. "My God!" That was Bedwyr. Just ahead, Hywel checked his horse.

Exhilarated by the heat of battle, Goronwy threw back his head and laughed, and then he spurred his horse into the fray, Hywel and Bedwyr close behind. Even if this was his end, he would die with his friends. He put everything from his mind but his sword and the men he intended to kill with it.

He met a Mercian axe with his blade and ripped it away. He turned to the other side and thrust the point through another man's throat. But then a third man buried his axe in his horse's chest, and the creature went down. Goronwy cleared his feet from the stirrups just in time. Back to back with Hywel, with hardly a pause for breath, he continued to fight.

Sweat poured down his face as Goronwy shoved his sword through the midsection of one Mercian, pulled it from his belly, and in almost the same motion, slashed through another's thigh. He spun and met a third man's blade. A grin split the red-bearded Mercian's face. For the first time, Goronwy felt weakness in his arms and found himself giving way under the onslaught.

And then the point of an arrow punched through the Mercian's ribs. He'd been lunging at Goronwy, his axe held above his head and ready for a killing blow. Instead, from her vantage point at the top of the keep, Rhiann had shot him.

Behind Goronwy, Hywel fought on as one possessed, and Goronwy resumed his place at his back. Sweat ran into Goronwy's eyes, and he swiped at it with the back of his hand. Or maybe those were tears.

They'd been tears, in fact, of pain and rage at what the Saxons had wrought. Now, as Goronwy stood on the battlements of Dinas Bran looking east, the sight of the banner of Mercia coming towards him nearly brought him to his knees. The memory of what they'd endured at Caer Fawr still clouded his vision, and he fought it. Men had died that day at King Penda's behest. That some of those deaths had been an illusion brought on by Mabon's *glamour*, did nothing to quell the fire in Goronwy's belly at what had happened to them there. Even now, three months on, most nights he dreamed of that battle.

When he was able to sleep at all.

He licked his lips at the bitter taste the vision had left in his mouth. The meddling of the *sidhe* represented nothing more or less than everything that was wrong with the world. Goronwy's stomach churned to think of the smug look of superiority that seemed a permanent fixture on Mabon's face. He hated the way Arianrhod, the goddess of the silver wheel of time and fate, manipulated mortals—Cade in particular, but that meant all those who served him—to do her bidding whether he wanted to or not. And it was a crime of the first order that Taliesin was beholden to Gwydion, Arianrhod's brother, for his *sight*, and found it conferred or withheld at the *sidhe's* whim.

Goronwy believed to the depths of his being that the world would be a better place without the *sidhe* in it, and yet—

A hand on his arm startled him, and he turned, the rage still untamed inside him. "What?"

Catrin stared at him wide-eyed. She took a step back, both hands coming up defensively. "I'm sorry, my lord. I didn't mean to disturb your thoughts."

Goronwy took in a deep breath, dampening down his emotions. These days his anger was never far from the surface. "It is I who should be sorry. You have done nothing wrong." He pointed over the battlement to the company of Mercians that had started to make its way up the long road from the valley floor. "I saw them coming and was thinking of Caer Fawr."

A shadow entered Catrin's eyes, for she'd been there too—not as a warrior but as the healer she was. "I'm sorry," she said again. "I wish I could help."

Coming from someone else, her words might have sounded patronizing, and the last thing Goronwy wanted was sympathy. But Catrin meant them exactly as she'd said them. She was also one of the reasons that his hatred of the world of the *sidhe* couldn't be sustained for long. For like Taliesin, she was a seer, though rather than seeing the future, she sensed magic and the truth in people.

Unfortunately for Goronwy, hating the world of the *sidhe* was also not far off from hating himself. His mother had been the great seeress, Nest, and he had inherited a small portion of her abilities. As a child he'd seen auras—the shimmer of light around a person ranging across the spectrum from purple to red, indicating good or evil, health or sickness. His mother had been extraordinarily pleased when she'd realized that he had inherited her gift. But the way she'd spoken of it—and him—to others had made Goronwy uncomfortable. He hadn't *wanted* to be a seer. He wanted to be a warrior.

Before long, he taught himself to turn his head away from what his inner eye showed him, and he refused to speak of it to her again. The first time he denied his gift, his mother had slapped his face. But any strong-willed child learns very quickly how to get the better of his parent, and denying his gift gained Goronwy attention—for a time. Then, of course, as his abilities disappeared, his mother lost all interest in him.

Whatever else Goronwy's mother had been, her gift had been a true one. Catrin reminded Goronwy very much of her, though Catrin's heart was warmer, despite her years of isolation, than his mother's had ever been. In the aftermath of Caer Fawr, it had occurred to him for the first time in many years that he might have done himself a disservice in suppressing his gift in favor of those feelings that came from his physical senses: the smooth leather of his sword hilt in his hand, the crunch of a man's nose breaking as Goronwy hit him with his elbow, or the smell of a woman's skin.

Those sensations, to him, were far more important and real than the world of the *sidhe*, but his familiarity with the ways of the gods was probably also one of the reasons he hadn't run away from Cade when he'd learned the truth about who he really was—or Catrin, for that matter, when he'd encountered her on the road from Caerleon. Hiding his sight had never troubled Goronwy because he'd told himself that he really was no different from anyone else. Any man could have the sight if he would only open himself up to it.

The more Goronwy dreamt of Caer Fawr, however, the more he was starting to think that maybe this wasn't entirely true.

He had accepted his preternatural awareness as part and parcel of what any good fighter could marshal when the need arose. Cade had it. Goronwy thought that even his younger brother, Dafydd, who was born of a different mother from Goronwy, had it. But if Goronwy was honest with himself, he had to admit that his gifts went beyond the usual, and to attribute his skill in battle to training alone was the worst of hubris, of the kind the *sidhe* would frown upon most severely.

It was as if, after all his years of adventuring and wandering, he'd come full circle.

Catrin lifted her chin to indicate the oncoming Mercians. "Why would Penda be coming here?"

Goronwy looked with her. "I doubt it's Penda. Peada at best, or perhaps a lesser lord who does Penda's bidding. Regardless, Penda should know better than to show his face in Cade's court ever again."

The rage threatened to overwhelm Goronwy once again, but even as he fought it, he found Catrin's hand resting on his arm as she'd done before he'd shouted at her. "I know anger can help men in battle, and it is hard to let go of once you've left the field, but I see how it eats away at you. Can I help?"

Goronwy almost growled at her again, but he swallowed that down too. "I don't need help. I have it under control." But even as he spoke, he knew his words weren't true, by the very fact of his denial.

She didn't argue with him, just studied him with that gentle expression. He cleared his throat, knowing that if he looked into those gray eyes for another heartbeat, he'd be back to tears, and that he couldn't have—not with Mercia on their doorstep. So instead of answering or being honest, he cleared his throat, gave her a stiff bow, and departed for the gatehouse.

As he strode away, he deliberately put Catrin from his mind. With four days to Cade's crowning, the last thing he needed was to be distracted by her or his own emotions. A warrior learned to accept his role in the order of things and to live with the consequences of his actions—or he didn't live long.

* * * * *

Catrin watched Goronwy stride towards the gatehouse where undoubtedly he would be one of the first to inspect whoever this was who was riding to Dinas Bran on behalf of King Penda. For months Catrin been trying to reach Goronwy, and with this latest rejection, she finally had to accept that she'd tried for the last time. All she'd wanted to tell him was that she sensed a great foreboding in the mountain beneath their feet. It had been growing in her mind for some time, though she hadn't put into words what she was sensing. It was very real to her now, however, and her thought had been to discuss it first with Goronwy before going to Taliesin or Cade.

When they'd met, she'd dismissed Goronwy as a soldier, who was by definition an oaf and not worthy of her time. Months of association had shown her that he was a prince and a warrior, with a sharp mind that understood far more than he let on. Even more, he was an honorable man, with a sense of humor and a large heart which he hid beneath a polished exterior.

Catrin looked down at her feet. She'd been alone for a long time, and for years she'd told herself that no man would ever move her again. At Caer Fawr, she'd wondered if walking at Taliesin's side might be one kind of end for her, but before he'd departed on his quest for the Thirteen Treasures of Britain, he'd made it clear to her that they were not meant to be together, and she had bowed to his wishes and his wisdom.

After that, it had been natural for her to turn to Goronwy for companionship. He wasn't afraid of her like so many others and, on rare occasions, she'd even sensed a kind of magic in him—though that didn't happen often. And when he was angry, as he'd been just now, he was no different from any other mortal man.

After Caer Fawr, if she'd asked, Cade would have ensured a safe journey for her to wherever she wanted to go. He had men who served him all across north Wales, any one of whom would have been delighted to find themselves housing a gifted healer.

But she'd stayed, and as Catrin gazed at the oncoming Mercians, she realized that doing so had been a mistake. Before she'd come north with Goronwy, she'd been able to feel the hum of the earth in everything she touched. But since she'd arrived at Cade's court, she'd felt disconnected from life around her. At first she'd thought it was because she'd spent too much time inside the castle, separated from the earth by the rocky outcrop on which the castle perched.

But then Catrin realized that her disengagement didn't have anything to do with whether it was rock or soil beneath her feet. She was a seer, and the earth was a living, breathing thing that a few feet of stone, which were part of the earth too, could hardly affect. No, it had to do with allowing others to choose her path for her.

It was time to go, and maybe it would make sense to go now. She would tell Cade about the darkness rising within the mountain, let Rhiann know that she was leaving, and then slip out the wicket gate. With the arrival of the Mercians and the ongoing preparations for Cade's departure for Caer Fawr tomorrow night, nobody—and by that she could admit she meant Goronwy—would even notice she was gone. Before she could think better of her decision, she hurried from the battlement to find Cade and Rhiann, and then to collect her things.

2

Rhiann

Rhiann glared at her husband, her hands on her hips. "You didn't really think this was going to be easy, did you?"

Cade laughed, his whole body shaking with amusement. "I was a fool, Rhiann. Forgive me?"

Rhiann shook her head. *As if there was anything to forgive.* "Now, what about Llywelyn?"

"I've known too many who've gone back on their word to choose that name," Cade said.

Rhiann collapsed onto a nearby stool. "You have known far too many men who've disgraced their honor. How are we to choose a name when you eliminate every one for that reason?"

"Our son, if I am not mistaken that this child is to be a son, is going to have enough to live up to—or live down to—without being burdened by an inappropriate name."

Rhiann eyed him. "How likely is it that you are wrong about the child being a boy?"

Cade looked down at the ground. Rhiann knew that stance. He looked down when he was struggling with himself—in this case because he didn't want to appear arrogant, even though he would be lying if he said that there was a possibility he didn't know for certain.

She made a *huh* sound at the back of her throat. It wasn't that she didn't want a son. While she knew that Cade would be pleased by a daughter—and would say so if asked—every man *needed* a son, especially a man who would soon be crowned High King of the Britons. Not even three months in the womb, and the child was already burdened with the kingship. "Then I suppose Cadfael won't work. I would so like to name our son after my father."

Cade glanced up, his face paling, but then he saw the smile twitching on Rhiann's lips. "You had me worried for a moment."

"I wouldn't be opposed to Cadwallon," Rhiann said.

"It may come to that, though Cadwallon ap Cadwaladr ap Cadwallon is quite a mouthful to foist on a child."

"I'm sure we'd manage. We'd call him *Wally*." Rhiann grinned outright at how Cade's face paled again. "Then again, he will be born at Christmas. We could call him—"

A knock came at the door, interrupting Rhiann's next suggestion. It was probably just as well, because Cade wouldn't have liked the name on her lips any more than he'd liked any of the others.

"Come in," Cade said.

Taliesin pushed the door open wide enough to poke his head in the space between the frame and the door. At Cade's impatient wave, he shoved the door open fully. The bard was wearing his ratty old cloak and traveling boots—and a pack on his back.

Rhiann frowned. "We aren't leaving until tomorrow. Why are you already dressed for a journey now?"

"Because I'm going away," Taliesin said. "Alone."

Unhappiness rose in Rhiann's chest. Catrin had just informed them that she couldn't stay another hour at Dinas Bran, and now Taliesin looked to be telling them the same thing. Cade, however, seemed completely unsurprised by this news. "I will not try to stop you. May God show you the straight path." He canted his head. "Or the gods, if you prefer."

"I can guarantee you that my path will not be straight." Taliesin released a puff of air. "Up until Caer Fawr, we were luckier than maybe we deserved or was warranted, but everything I've discovered since then has only made me more fearful of what we face."

Cade nodded. "A moment ago, Catrin told me that she sensed power shifting within the mountain. Is that what is sending you away?"

"I was leaving already." He looked directly at Cade. "You should too."

"I had planned to leave for Caer Fawr tomorrow night," Cade said.

"No. Now."

That was unusually straightforward speaking for Taliesin. Cade looked at him for a heartbeat, but then he nodded, accepting his bluntness as urgency. "All right. We will." He grimaced. "After I speak to whoever is coming to see me from Mercia."

Rhiann rose to her feet and put her arms around Taliesin in a quick embrace. He didn't respond, just stood where he was planted, unbending as a tree. "Thank you," she released him, "for everything." She hadn't expected him to hug her back. It wasn't his way, and she didn't take offense.

"I will return, my dear." Then Taliesin smiled—that joyful, child-like smile that made him look younger than she was, even though she knew he was very old inside. "I already promised your husband that I would."

"I know that too," Rhiann said. "I expect to see you again, but sometimes you get lost, and I didn't want you to go without telling you how I felt."

Taliesin had left them shortly after the battle at Caer Fawr and spent the intervening months searching for the Thirteen Treasures of Britain. Everywhere he went, he found other men ahead of him or just behind, but in every case, he'd found no sign of the remaining Treasures. On one hand, that could be construed as a comfort, but on the other, if the Treasures were being moved or hidden, then the one doing so was growing more powerful by the day.

Taliesin kept the smile on his face, though it became a little fixed at her frank expression of emotion. But then he bowed. She'd thrown in the comment about getting lost to let him know that he hadn't deceived her with his assurances. He was worried—about them, about Wales, and about the darkness beneath their feet.

His arms folded across his chest, Cade had continued to study Taliesin throughout his exchange with Rhiann. "*Cariad,* will you excuse us?"

Rhiann nodded and left the room, closing the door gently behind her. Cade and Taliesin communicated on a level that left her out, but after everything she and Cade had been through, she'd learned to trust that he would tell her what he and Taliesin discussed when she needed to know.

She entered the great hall and pulled up short at the sight of the party of Mercians entering from the other direction through the front doors. They must have galloped up the mountain to have reached the castle already.

Striding ahead of his troop of ten men was Peada, the son of Penda, the King of Mercia. At her appearance, he stopped too, halting just past the central fireplace. The fire was burning brightly and drawing well, thanks to the blessing Taliesin had bestowed upon it—as well as the newly cleared vent in the right hand wall that brought air into the room and encouraged the smoke and ash to draw upwards towards the hole in the ceiling.

The glow of the flames lit Peada's face. "I would speak to your lord."

Rhiann found it difficult to even look at Peada. She was beyond angry at his father, who'd caused the deaths of so many Britons. The Mercians had been deceived by Mabon's whisperings, as had many men over the years, but the battle at Caer Fawr had been only one of a long string of outrages against the Welsh committed by Peada's people.

"Why?" she said, unwilling to even make the attempt to be polite.

Peada blinked. He hadn't expected to be challenged.

Rhiann took in a breath, reining in her temper, and gestured towards several small tables arranged near the fire. "Please, sit. The time for the evening meal has not yet come, but I will arrange for food for you. My husband is in close conference with his advisors, and I will let him know that you are here."

Peada's expression cleared at her explanation, and he bowed. "Thank you, Madam." Then he gestured to his men that they should fill in the benches on either side of the table.

Rhiann spun on her heel and marched back the way she'd come, heading towards the kitchen. She needed to let the cook know that a prince of Mercia and his men had entered the hall. It would be courteous, as Queen of Gwynedd, for her to serve him with her own hands, but she couldn't stomach the thought.

Fortunately, just as she reached the doorway, Cade and Taliesin appeared, coming from the side corridor, and Rhiann hastened to intercept them before they entered the hall. "It's Peada who has come!"

Cade put his arm around her waist and guided her around a corner, farther from the great hall. But when he spoke, his words were for Taliesin. "If you're going to go, my friend, you should go now, quickly, before we get bogged down in whatever bad news Peada has brought."

"If you need me to stay, my lord—"

"Of course I need you to stay," Cade said, "but your task is urgent—more urgent than anything Peada could need from me. I don't know what you can accomplish in the four days before my crowning, but if something is to be accomplished, it has to be now. There is nothing more important than that. If you really have pinpointed the force that has sent Mabon questing for the Treasures, we need to be the ones to get to them first."

"That's what you had to say to him?" Rhiann looked from Taliesin to Cade and back again. "You finally know who's behind this game that isn't a game?"

Taliesin looked directly at Rhiann, something he didn't very often do. She thought it was because he was wary of seeing into the eyes of any mortal, since in so doing, he would see far more than the mortal intended, and it would be a violation of his or her privacy. She didn't fear him knowing about her, however. She had secrets, as every woman did, but none were so terrible that she couldn't share them with him.

"Throughout the centuries, many have sought to gather the Thirteen Treasures of Britain. Mortals and immortals alike reach for power, but this time is different. It might be hubris on my part, but I trust myself with them more than anyone else."

"It isn't hubris, Taliesin," Rhiann said flatly. "None want, as you and Cade do, simply to protect them."

Cade's arm was still around her, and he squeezed her waist. "I'm glad you're so sure, *cariad*, though I am not." He gave a somewhat disparaging laugh—not directed at her but at himself. "I intend to use them as well. I would cut off my right hand before I'd give up Caledfwlch." He put a hand on the hilt of his sword. "It is a treasure as much as any of the others. Of course, I intend to use it only for good, to heal and protect, but I have killed with it too. Who's to say that my motives are purer than another man's?"

"They are," Rhiann said. "Your people attest to it."

"So I tell myself. So Taliesin tells me."

Taliesin pressed his lips together, thinking again before speaking. "I have never told you the full power of the Treasures, Rhiann, for the truth isn't for all ears. But you will be queen, and you carry Cade's heir, and perhaps it is time you knew the truth too."

"Too?" Rhiann glanced at Cade, who was looking very grave. This moment was exactly what she'd told herself that she trusted Cade and Taliesin enough to wait for—the moment when they told her what she needed to know.

"If we do not find the Treasures, Cade will be able to unite Wales for a time. But then, like all kings, no matter how great, he will fail and his kingdom will fall. Death is a fate accorded to all men, of course, but your husband is special. He is the heir to Arthur, the successor the stars have foretold for over a century. Even more, Wales faces many challenges in the coming years. If we do not gather the Treasures now, while they are in play, they will disappear again." With uncharacteristic ferocity, Taliesin clenched his right hand into a fist and pounded it into his left. "Hundreds of years from now Wales will suffer grievously—"

"At the hand of the Saxons?" Rhiann said, horrified to hear that all their sacrifices would come to nothing.

"By them, yes, but they will be in the service of a new invader, a powerful overlord whom the world does not yet know. If we have the Treasures, their power will still protect us. Even at the last end of need, they will remind our blood that we are Welsh, and through their power, we will always find the strength to rise again."

Rhiann looked at him closely. She didn't know that she'd ever seen such a determined look on his face. "You mean that, don't you?"

Cade grimaced. "He has seen many things."

"Defeat?" Rhiann said.

"Of course," Taliesin said. "Defeat is always on the horizon. What I fear more, however, is the black hand that attempts to wipe our people from the earth: our language, our culture, our laws ... there is no future where that hammer does not fall on us. But if we have the Treasures, he might take our lands from us, but he will never take our hearts."

Rhiann's face was pale, and she put her hand on her belly, fearing for her unborn child and what he would face.

"The next four days are critical because I sense my opponent's power growing. He wants that future to come to pass, and he fears Cade and his crowning."

"Why?" Rhiann said.

"Because the crowning of a High King becomes a locus of all the powers of the ancients." Taliesin spoke as if it were obvious. "I despair to think that the old ways are so forgotten that men today think the purpose of naming a High King is to choose a battle leader." He scoffed.

"Do you think this power will try to disrupt my crowning?" Cade said.

"I'm certain of it," Taliesin said. "It is why I have not named him and won't. Not until I'm sure it is really he."

Cade let out a sharp breath. "You don't comfort me."

"Good, since I didn't mean to." Taliesin bobbed his head. "I've had a vision of what you are facing at Peada's behest. I'm leaving because, in the vision, I was there instead of elsewhere, and the outcome was—" he paused, searching for the appropriate word, "—undesirable."

Rhiann and Cade stared at him. It was strange to hear of their tumultuous future standing in a simple corridor.

"Goodbye for now, my lord. My lady." Taliesin turned abruptly and strode away from them.

Rhiann tried not to gape at the words he'd left them with, and then caught between horror and disbelief, she looked up at Cade. "What did he mean about *undesirable*? And who is this powerful being he fears so much? *Who has been driving Mabon all this time?*"

"I don't know. I think Taliesin desperately wants to be wrong, and he fears the power of the name. To speak it would draw our enemy to us." Cade made a motion with one hand, not dismissing their conversation with Taliesin, but moving on from it. "Now … why is Peada here?"

"I don't know what he wants. Taliesin didn't tell you what future he saw regarding these Mercians either?"

Cade laughed. "Of course not. The man prides himself on being obscure, though he has been more frank with us today than he ever has. That alone should tell us how dangerous the path we walk is. Then again, seeing the future—or many possible futures—is a burden I wouldn't want to carry. He left because the future he saw when he stayed was worse."

Rhiann shook her head. "It was clear that going was hardly better."

Cade reached for Rhiann's hand and squeezed. "I don't need Taliesin's foresight to know what Peada wants. Uncle Penda wants my help. He has reconsidered what I told him on the battlefield at Caer Fawr—that I will not fight at his side—and decided that he cannot take no for an answer. It was only a matter of time before Oswin of Northumbria made another foray into Mercia. Penda defeated the first attempt, but that was due to luck more than skill."

Rhiann canted her head. "I've heard you say that wise men make their own luck."

"They do." Cade's arm came around her as he guided her towards the great hall. "But Peada is here because his father is wise not to think he can rely on luck a second time, and that his luck might have finally run out. I'm thinking that he wants a bit of mine."

3

Dyrnwyn, the flaming sword, lost for centuries beneath the earth.
A hamper that feeds a hundred, a knife to serve twenty-four,
A chariot to carry a man on the wind,
A halter to tame any horse.
The cauldron of the Giant to test the brave,
A whetstone for deadly sharpened swords,
An entertaining chess set,
A crock and a dish, each to fill one's every wish,
A drinking horn that bestows immortality to those worthy of it,
And the mantle of Arthur.
His healing sword descends;
Our enemies flee our unseen and mighty champion.

—Taliesin,
The Thirteen Treasures of Britain,
The Black Book of Gwynedd

Taliesin

Taliesin checked his pack one more time, taking note that it still contained the green cloak he'd worn to Cade and Rhiann's wedding. The color matched his eyes, and while he might pay later for that bit of vanity, he didn't leave it behind. Even a seer might need extra warmth on a cold night.

He slung the pack over his shoulder and allowed the side door of the keep to hit his back as it swung gently closed behind him. He stood in the shadow of the wall, testing the currents in the air for the menace that Catrin had spoken of. Now that another had felt it, he knew he couldn't dismiss it another moment, and his stomach clenched. Though he had been leaving already—he'd told Cade the truth about that—the evil was pushing him out the door, even when he feared what might result from his leaving.

Taliesin had seen desolation overtake the world if he didn't renew this quest. But that didn't mean that the immediate danger to Cade was any less significant. Everywhere Taliesin turned he saw carnage, death, and despair. Navigating through his visions along a path that brought the least danger and the best outcome was taxing him to the limits of his ability.

Still, he took in a breath as the sweet evening air wafted through the fort. No evil twisted on the currents. Neither was there a sign of any immediate threat—not even from the Mercian men and horses that filled the courtyard and hall. The kitchen workers would be run off their feet between now and when Cade's company left for Caer Fawr later this evening. The last thing they needed was more mouths to feed, but Cade would deal with Peada as a king's son deserved. That task was not beyond him or Rhiann. Of that, Taliesin was sure, even if he was certain of little else. Cade would be faced with equally dangerous allies for as long as he ruled Wales.

Despite the danger that lay ahead and the urgency that pressed on him, telling Taliesin to *get on with it*, his heart lifted. In his mind's eye, he saw the road beckoning to him once again. He had spent most of the last three months since the battle at Caer Fawr chasing rumors of the Treasures. Back in March, he'd set out with high hopes, but as the weeks of travel had worn on, his failure had begun to weigh on him, to the point that he'd eventually retraced his steps and returned to Dinas Bran. The news that the Treasures had surfaced had spread far and wide, and many men dreamed of the power even one item could bring them. Fortunately, most only knew of the rumors, not of the reality, and more of Taliesin's time had been spent putting rumor to rest than in actual searching.

Perhaps it was hubris for Taliesin, who could occasionally straddle the divide between the world of the *sidhe* and this one, to set himself this task, but his travels these last months had shown him that the Treasures were in motion. While Cade would become High King with or without the remaining items, the honor would be a hollow one if the Treasures were still in play.

For they wanted to be together, and to gather them under Cade's dragon banner was worth any cost. Even Taliesin's life. With only four days left until Cade's crowning, it was looking more and more like such sacrifice might be necessary.

That was one future Taliesin saw. There were others.

The possible avenues of what might be came to him in a mass of impression, though he could make out individual scenes too. In one thread, he saw Cade putting his sword through Penda's belly. In another, he saw Goronwy sweeping Catrin into his arms—and the possibility made Taliesin smile. At one time Catrin had fancied him, but Taliesin knew that his path diverged from hers. A dozen other possible futures, all equally likely and unlikely, spread out before him. He'd spoken to Cade and Rhiann of the worst future, but there were many others in which the enemies of the Welsh rolled over Wales like a cart downhill. What faced his people was bad enough even if Cade did succeed in uniting the Treasures. Without them, it would catastrophic.

Initially, Cade had gathered the Treasures to him in order to prevent the child-god, Mabon, from gaining complete power in the world of the *sidhe*. The fact that Cade had succeeded in stopping Mabon didn't mean the threat was over, however. Mabon still sought power, but Taliesin had seen no sign of him these last months. In fact, he hadn't seen any sign of any *sidhe*, benevolent, malicious, or otherwise. Even the woods had been devoid of demons. Cade's war band had killed many monsters in the months before Caer Fawr, but still, their absence was almost more worrying than their presence.

In the lines of the future that continued from this moment, Taliesin saw mostly loss and failure. What made him put one foot in front of the other, however, were those few instances of joy, of laughter, and of genuine happiness. He held onto those visions. It mattered not that they were few and far between. As long as there was hope, he would keep fighting. It went without saying that Cade and his companions felt the same.

Out of thirteen Treasures, they currently had knowledge or possession of seven. Perhaps the most powerful lay beneath Dinas Bran. This was the Cup of Christ, known to the druids as a drinking horn. At one time Taliesin had refused to acknowledge that the horn and the Cup were one and the same, though he saw that truth plainly now. Because of its location, to Taliesin's mind, it belonged to Cade, and both men were content that it should remain hidden forever. The Christian god—Cade's god—had combined with Taliesin's own efforts to hold back the darkness beneath Dinas Bran. He'd meditated long on this fact but had come to no satisfactory conclusion as to the how or why of what had happened in the cavern. His only recourse had been to accept, for now, what was.

Cade also possessed the mantle, which allowed him to walk unharmed under the sun, though it also made him invisible to the mortal eye; Caledfwlch, his healing sword taken from Castle Ddu; Dyrnwyn, the flaming sword Arawn himself had once borne; the knife; the whetstone; and a single chess piece with which Mabon had teased Rhiann. The last of the seven, the cauldron, resided in the caverns beneath Caer Dathyl in the possession of Cade's cousin,

Gwyn. As Gwyn himself had said, he was bound to the cauldron and it to him, and his allegiance was to Cade. Like the cup, Taliesin believed it safe from all comers.

That left six remaining to find: the hamper, the crock, the dish, the halter, the chariot, and the chess set, the gathering of which might be a Herculean task all by itself. Taliesin mocked himself at the thought. He'd lived lifetimes of men, but it seemed that all would rise or fall on this one.

As he'd warned Cade and Rhiann, someone was gathering power to himself. Taliesin hadn't given Cade the name because names had power—and in this case, naming the god Efnysien would do more than call down his wrath—it would strike fear into the heart of every soul who heard it. Efnysien's long list of atrocities made the activities of Mabon look positively benign.

"You're leaving too?" Catrin stepped from behind a post near Dinas Bran's wicket gate. Peada's men had moved on, away from the gatehouse towards the stable and barracks, so she and Taliesin were alone.

"I am."

"I'm coming with you," Catrin said.

"My dear, you are not—"

"Why would you stop me? You've had so much luck all alone that you think repeating the same mistake will bring a different outcome, even at this late hour?"

It was a cool day for June, and Catrin was dressed appropriately for a journey, with a cloak and pack of her own. Her soot-black hair, lithe body, and gray eyes seemed to penetrate to Taliesin's core at times. He didn't know that he could have said that of any other person, man or woman—not even Cade, who shared Taliesin's connection with the world of the *sidhe*.

"I like talking to myself," Taliesin said, latching upon the one item in her list she couldn't counter.

"And you sleep with one eye open?" Catrin said.

"I'm not defenseless just because I don't bear a sword."

"I would never suggest—"

But another voice cut her off before she could finish. "One woman, no matter how courageous, will not be enough to protect you, Taliesin." Goronwy stepped out of the shadows where he'd been standing by the gatehouse. "I'm coming too."

Goronwy, a warrior-prince in his own right and Cade's right-hand man, was dressed as usual in mail and cloak, girded with a sword and bristling with who-knew-how-many other weapons. At a minimum, he had a knife up each bracer and down both boots. His fair hair shone in the light of the torches in the courtyard, newly lit with the waning of the day. Although he wasn't as tall as either Dafydd or Taliesin, Goronwy loomed over Catrin. The only unusual addition to his appearance was the pack slung on his back.

"My friends—" Taliesin looked from Catrin to Goronwy, barely controlling his expression of dismay. He had thought that the work that he and Cade had done beneath the earth had restored his sight, but he hadn't had any inkling before this moment that these two would waylay him at the very start of his journey. In fact, in all of his visions of his future, he had never seen them at his side. He'd prepared himself for a solitary journey, whether or not that was what he'd wanted. "In the past, your company has not been unwelcome, but where I'm going now, you cannot protect me."

"I have never held Dyrnwyn," Goronwy said, "but that does not mean I am not worthy to travel with you. There are few things that frighten me, and no place that I will not follow you."

Taliesin felt uncomfortably besieged. He understood people's minds without conscious thought, but he'd never been very good at talking to them. "You—" He hesitated without finishing the thought. Goronwy wasn't wrong in the sense that, of all of Cade's companions, his lineage was the most ancient, since it adjoined with Cade's own, and his latent abilities as a seer would stand him well in the Otherworld, which was of course where Taliesin was going.

"If you won't let us come with you," Catrin said. "We will trail behind and protect you anyway."

"It won't be that easy to keep up with me," Taliesin said.

"That does not mean, however, that we wouldn't try," Goronwy said, "and if you lost us, you'd worry about us. Much better to consent to let us tag along."

Were they right? Were the sidhe playing him for a fool again? Taliesin gazed at his two friends. As they looked back at him, he pulled apart their personalities, their wants, and their desires. He had believed that he could see right through them, and yet, they had surprised him.

"You do realize that we're going to walk?" Taliesin said.

Goronwy let out a snort of disbelief. "Why would you do that?"

"Walking is slow, but it connects me to the earth. My mistake before was in thinking that I needed to hurry, and I allowed myself to become distracted. If I am to find the Treasures, I must feel them the only way I know how."

Catrin and Goronwy shared a brief glance, and then Goronwy shrugged. "So be it. He stuck out one foot. "I've had these boots for a while. They're worn and perfect for walking. Though," he added, "if you had a mind to ride, I wouldn't object."

"I don't want to be responsible for horses," Taliesin said. "The Treasures straddle the human world and that of the *sidhe,* and it is in the world of the *sidhe* that I have not yet looked."

Goronwy's chin firmed. "If you cross into the Otherworld, it is of no matter. I will follow you anywhere you lead."

Taliesin looked at Catrin. "And you?"

"I know I can be of some use to you," she said. "I have gifts that might aid you, even if they are weaker than your own."

"Different," Taliesin said, though he wasn't sure what made him clarify. "Just different from my own."

Catrin bowed her head in acknowledgement and then reached for the latch on the wicket gate that allowed travelers to pass in and out of Dinas Bran without opening the big double doors underneath the gatehouse.

"Just as long as you don't disturb my thoughts," Taliesin said.

"When have I ever?" Catrin said.

Without actually giving his assent, Taliesin passed through the wicket gate and stepped onto the path that wound down from Dinas Bran. The village of Llangollen lay at its base. Goronwy was right, of course, that riding would be faster. It would take them an hour to reach the valley floor, rather than a quarter of that time by horseback. But Taliesin knew that he was right too. He needed the hum of the earth beneath his feet as he walked.

As a child he'd gone without shoes as part of his training. His adult form was heavier, however, and though Taliesin was loath to admit it, the soles of his feet had softened since last summer. He promised himself that when he completed this task, if he ever completed it, he would find a cottage in the mountains and run barefoot every day.

Taliesin eyed Catrin. She might be a barefoot person too. In fact, at that very moment, a vision came to him of her dancing in a meadow, arms wide, with mountain flowers beneath her feet and her dress spinning out around her. He allowed the vision to draw him in for just a moment before suppressing it. He knew without question that it was a true seeing and one of the moments of joy that pulled him forward. Then he looked past Catrin to Goronwy, who was bringing up the rear, trying to imagine him barefoot. It was impossible, and Taliesin had a moment of amusement to think that if anyone could transform Goronwy it was Catrin.

The trio stumped along down the road. At first they encountered a dozen common folk returning to the castle after working in the fields or pastures for the day, but by the time they were halfway down the mountain, it was nearing full dark, and they passed no other soul. Taliesin muttered the incantation that lit the end of his staff, putting enough into it so all three of them could clearly see the path ahead.

Mostly they walked in silence, except for occasional mutters from Goronwy—complaints of one kind or another, jokes for Catrin's amusement, or comments on the day. Such was his way. Throughout every journey Taliesin had experienced with Goronwy, he and Bedwyr, who more often than not was Goronwy's foil, had maintained a near constant stream of humor and goodwill, belying their outward gruffness.

It didn't take long, however, for Goronwy to need a response from someone other than himself. "How, by the way, are we going to reach the Otherworld?"

"That wasn't a question you thought to ask before you decided to come along?" Taliesin said.

Grumble, grumble. "I'm asking it now—"

But Goronwy was unable to finish his sentence because the earth shifted beneath their feet. Between one heartbeat and the next, instead of standing on the beaten dirt of the path, Taliesin found himself in a bowl-shaped cavern. Before him rose a light that blinded him at the same time that it pierced him to his core. Out of the light stepped the raven-haired goddess, Arianrhod. Her brother Gwydion, Taliesin's patron, stood beside her. They were siblings—and looked it—with black hair and blue eyes, but to describe them thus was to do them a disservice. For their hair and eyes—and entire beings—were indescribable in their beauty. Taliesin's mind, once given the task, shied away from it.

He bowed. "My lady. My lord."

"Taliesin," Gwydion said.

Arianrhod held out a hand to the bard. Tentatively, Taliesin stepped forward, not daring to think that she wanted him to actually touch her. She didn't drop her hand, however, and continued to regard him steadily, so he touched the tips of his fingers to hers. A shock passed through him, and his body vibrated from head to toe.

Arianrhod nodded and dropped her hand.

Taliesin bowed again, shivering though the evening air wasn't cold. "Is it possible that I may serve you?"

"You may," Arianrhod said.

Dread surged through him. Taliesin had said the words out of obedience, allegiance, and awe of the moment, hoping against hope that she would not take him up on his offer. What could a *sidhe* ask of a human, even one as old as Taliesin? Then, from within the light, another figure formed and stepped out from behind Arianrhod and Gwydion. Like his mother, he had transformed himself into the human conception of beauty, with the same black hair and blue eyes that marked him as a Celt, though he was no Celt. He was the god, Mabon.

Taliesin's jaw clenched. One could hardly speak of a god as having character—certainly Mabon was without a soul—but the absence of both in Mabon was a pronounced and dangerous weakness. Cade despised him, and Mabon knew of this disdain—and knew too that Cade's companions shared his opinion. If Taliesin had allowed himself an opinion, he would have felt the same. As it was, he was a bard and a *gweledydd*, a seer, and such opinions were not a luxury he could afford. Still, few greater sins existed in the eyes of a *sidhe* than for a human to be anything but worshipful.

Behind him, Taliesin heard Goronwy snort under his breath.

Taliesin couldn't see the knight, since Goronwy and Catrin stood together, somewhere near rim of the cavern, but Taliesin didn't have to see Goronwy to feel the less than subtle mockery he was directing at Mabon. Taliesin would have turned and made a cutting motion with his hand, but he didn't dare move or lift his eyes from the ground.

"The council has spoken," Arianrhod said. "My son must leave our world for a time and walk among you as one of you. I would ask that you look after him, Taliesin."

Indescribable horror filled Taliesin, and he lifted his head to gaze at the goddess, a protest on his lips. Goronwy could mock and make snide comments as he wished, but Taliesin could feel the power coming from Mabon and knew what a terrible threat to the human world he represented. In that moment, Taliesin couldn't imagine a worse fate that being responsible for this wayward son of Cade's patroness.

Sidhe didn't live by the same rules as humans did. Some genuinely cared for humanity, but they were ultimately accountable only to the ruler of the gods, Beli, and his council, upon which both Gwydion and Arianrhod sat. For most, the threat of banishment was the only thing keeping them in line and had to substitute for an actual sense of morality. Mabon had defied them and was now paying the price for his ambition. For reasons Taliesin didn't understand, Efnysien was in another category entirely. Like Mabon, he was Beli's grandson, though by his daughter Penarddun. Unlike Mabon, however, the council never punished him, no matter how grievous his offenses, murder and betrayal among them.

Either Arianrhod didn't notice Taliesin's horror, didn't care, or had spent too little time in the human world to read Taliesin's emotions. He struggled to control his expression so she wouldn't guess what he was thinking.

"Furthermore, my father has decreed that the human world must be punished for its lack of faith. No longer do the people look to us, we who have provided for and aided them for so long. No longer do the old ways hold true. None of us are permitted to consort with you until my father deems the time has come to lift his ban."

"But—" Taliesin took an involuntary step towards Arianrhod. She didn't reject him, but her face turned as fixed as iron. Taliesin had been going to say that this was a completely wrong step. Humans craved guidance. If they couldn't get it from the *sidhe*, or if the *sidhe* were deemed capricious or unhelpful, they would turn even more to the Christian God, whom Cade said always listened, even if the answer wasn't necessarily what the petitioner wanted to hear.

Taliesin's eyes went to Gwydion. His patron was gazing straight ahead, but in a single instant, his eyes flicked to Taliesin's face, and he canted his head a tiny degree to his right. Taliesin tried not to gape at him. *What is he trying to tell me?*

Taliesin gritted his teeth and stepped back. "My lady." But even as he prepared to be dismissed, his eyes were drawn to the wall of the cavern, which Gwydion had indicated a moment before. The stylized images of a queen, a castle, and a rearing horse were drawn on the wall. If the rearing horse was meant to represent a knight, the three images could be chess pieces.

Then Arianrhod, Gwydion, and the cavern vanished, taking their illusion with them, and leaving Mabon standing alone in the road. The god placed his hands on his hips and grinned. "So, we're going to be together for a while. I think this sojourn in the human world might turn out to be quite fun!"

As Mabon smirked at the companions, Taliesin's stomach twisted yet again. It wasn't, however, because Arianrhod had foisted her son on them. By comparison to what Gwydion had just shown him, it was a small thing. What had him staring back at Mabon in dismay was the realization that the rearing horse was indeed meant to represent a chess piece, but it was also the personal badge of Efnysien.

4

Cade

Cade had suggested to Rhiann that she not make herself a target of Peada's scorn. Since she had no desire to be in the same room with the feckless Saxon ever again, she had willingly forgone the opportunity and departed for their quarters. Dinner was still a while off, and she could nap beforehand. Because nighttime was Cade's purview, he tended to keep her up late. Whether because he knew Cade's habits by now or by pure accident, Peada had arrived with the setting sun.

Taliesin had told Cade not to allow Penda's and Peada's acceptance of Mabon's authority to color his understanding of the men too much. Mabon had bent far stronger men than they to his will—and had been doing so since the beginning of time. While it was Peada's fault he was a coward—a fact for which Cade could not forgive him—he was Cade's cousin, the son of the King of Mercia, and thus someone Cade could neither dismiss nor ignore.

"Why are you here?" Cade halted at the head of the table near the fire where Peada and his men were sitting. They'd been served food and drink, though not by Rhiann's hand. Cade was glad that she'd had the courage to defy convention in this. What was the point of being the Queen of Gwynedd if at times you couldn't do what you wanted?

"After the battle before Caer Fawr, my father asked if you would fight with him." Peada paused to study Cade's face. For the first time in Cade's acquaintance, his look showed no superiority. Instead he appeared apprehensive. "What you may not know is that Oswin's new army is even larger than the one he threw against us after Caer Fawr. We barely held them off that time. We won't be able to do it again."

Cade took a chair from beside the fire and sat, his eyes never leaving Peada's face. "After Caer Fawr, your father wouldn't have held them off at all if not for the stomach sickness that swept through Northumbria. Oswin himself nearly died."

Peada made a dismissive motion with his hand, not denying the obvious truth, but not interested in discussing the past. "My father has sent me to ask you again to aid him, even to beg."

The last word came out of Peada's mouth a little unsteadily, as if the very idea of begging was an anathema to him. It would have been to Cade too, so he didn't begrudge Peada's reluctance to speak as he had.

What Peada didn't know was that Taliesin had told Cade, in one of his rare moments of candor when he gave real advice instead of cryptic warnings, that there was nothing Cade could do for Penda except die among his army. The King of Mercia was doomed, if not this week or this month, then by the end of the year. So was Peada, but not as soon and for a different reason: shortly after the defeat at Caer Fawr, he had married Oswin's own daughter, and it would be by her hand that he would eventually be brought down.

Oswin wanted the whole of Saxon England, and he had no qualms whatsoever about doing what he deemed necessary to take it. In fact, he viewed the gift of his daughter to Peada as a sign that Peada was now his servant. In Oswin's eyes, Mercia was an extension of Northumbria now, and he was marching to war not as one king challenging another, but to bring Peada and Penda to heel.

In turn, for Cade, refusing to aid Penda wasn't without consequences: if Cade let Mercia fall to Northumbria, Wales could be next. Of course, if Taliesin was right—and in this

Cade would not question him—it was only a matter of time before Mercia fell no matter what Cade did. And if Cade and his men fought and died for a lost cause, there would be nobody left to defend Wales.

"My father asks, at the very least, if you would be willing to meet with him, uncle to nephew and king to king," Peada said. "In fact, it would be our preference that you came with me tonight."

Cade didn't actually scoff out loud, but he was unable to keep his disbelief from his voice. "Tonight? You want me to ride with you tonight? To where?"

"Chester."

Chester was a city that had long been a seat of power—first for the ancient Britons; then for the Romans, who'd made it their capitol in the north of Britain; then for the rulers of Rheged during the time of Arthur; and now for the Mercians. Set within the curve of the River Dee on its eastern bank, Chester protected Mercia from incursions across the border from Gwynedd. Cadfael, Rhiann's father, had coveted the city, but like the men who'd ruled Gwynedd before him, he had never taken it.

"You want me to ride to Chester only four days from my crowning?"

Peada's begging aside, this request alone was enough to show Cade how desperate Penda had become.

"What better time? Meet him in the morning, and you can ride south to Caer Fawr immediately afterwards." Peada spoke reasonably enough, but then he followed up his earnest request with a sneer and a scoff. "I know why you chose to accept the crown of the Britons there, but it's hardly subtle."

"It wasn't meant to be." His elbow on the arm of his chair and a finger tapping his lips, Cade studied his cousin through a count of five. "It is bold of your father to ask me to walk into the lion's den."

Peada's face paled. "You know that my father doesn't believe."

"Not even now that you do?" Cade had expected that his cousin would understand the Biblical reference, since he'd converted to Christianity at his wife's request when he married her.

"That is half the reason Oswin has targeted my father's kingdom above any other. His priests tell him that all must follow the path of the Christ, and if he cannot convert them with words, then it must be by the sword."

"How Christian of them," Cade said dryly.

Peada shook his head. "I confess, cousin, that my new faith is shaken when I think back to the events at Caer Fawr."

"Why would that be?"

Peada flung out a hand. "Demons came forth from the Underworld, led by the god, Mabon! How can you believe in the Christ after what you've seen with your own eyes?"

"Just because Mabon exists does not mean the Christ did not die for our sins," Cade said patiently. "Faith is a matter of believing even when you don't have proof."

"Yes, but—"

"Did we not win?" Cade said.

Peada stared at him.

"Mabon is more powerful than any human, but his concerns are not ours. He cares only about himself," Cade said. "Christ claims dominion over the human heart and soul, neither of which are of any concern to Mabon—or the rest of the *sidhe*."

Peada spoke around a tightly clenched jaw. "My wife's priests refuse to believe that any of what I saw happened."

"That's their blindness." Cade leaned forward. "Will worshipping Mabon change his course? Does he in any way care about your adulation or bestow kindnesses on you—or your father for that matter—because you believe?"

Peada deflated. "No."

"You're worried about the wrong things, cousin," Cade said. "Mabon might want to use you, but he doesn't love you, and he can offer you nothing beyond the impermanence of this world."

Peada rose to his feet and bowed. "You should have been a priest, cousin. Your words are far more comforting than theirs." He hesitated. "Will you come?"

The very idea that Cade could say anything that might comfort Peada was disconcerting. Comforting Peada hadn't been Cade's intent, and he was thrown somewhat off-kilter by Peada's sudden camaraderie and respect. Cade didn't want to be friends with Peada, and he was so used to distrusting this Saxon cousin that he immediately reviewed everything that had passed between them with a measure of suspicion.

So instead of agreeing, he stalled. "Why do you not ask to meet at your father's castle at Westune? It is better fortified than Chester to withstand an assault by Oswin. Chester's walls encompass far too large a space and require at least two hundred men to properly defend."

"Because Chester contains the secret of my father's power," Peada said.

"How so?"

"The dish that caught the blood of Christ lies within its walls."

Cade gaped at him. "You tell me truly? You have seen it?"

Peada put out a hand. "No, not yet, but we know it's there—somewhere. God will bestow victory on whichever army possesses it, and I intend that army to be mine."

Cade settled back in his chair. "Your father should care little for Christian myth, Peada. Does Penda know about your quest?"

Peada laughed. "He leads it! Christian or pagan, it matters not. It is a Treasure, and sacred to all."

Cade found himself swallowing hard. As with the Cup of Christ buried beneath Dinas Bran, the pagan and Christian traditions coincided in this instance too. Many had sought the dish that had caught Christ's blood, and Cade would do everything in his power to prevent it from falling into the hands of any other creature—man or *sidhe*.

Cade had still been of two minds about whether he would hear Penda out, but Peada's news decided him. "I will come to Chester, but on my own terms. I had intended to leave tonight for Caer Fawr. After my crowning, I will ride to Chester and speak to your father."

"By then it will be too late."

Cade looked at him steadily. Even though Cade didn't mean to reveal himself in that moment, something of the power inside him must have showed, because Peada's face paled, and he bowed. "So be it. I wished for more, but the High King of the Britons has spoken."

5

Goronwy

Mabon continued to grin at them. "Well, are we going or not?"

Taliesin looked as if a litter of cats was fighting inside his head. If the little Goronwy knew about Taliesin's gift was true, that description might not be far off. But the fact that Goronwy appeared to be recovering from the shock of the *sidhe's* appearance quicker than Taliesin was perhaps more unsettling than the meeting itself.

"The goddess cannot be serious." Goronwy took in a deep breath and let it out, allowing the tension to ease out of him along with the air.

Catrin was equally horrified. "How can we possibly bring him with us? How could Arianrhod give her son to you, knowing as she must how much trouble he's caused us? He saw to the murder of Rhiann's father! He almost saw to the death of every one of us—not to mention Cade's entire army."

Goronwy added, somewhat less passionately, "Has she sent him to be a spy in our camp?"

Catrin shook her head. "Why would she need a spy? She's a *sidhe*." She put a hand on Taliesin's arm. "She is forbidden to interact with us. Does that mean she can't see us anymore either?"

Taliesin came out of his reverie, though his eyes were still on Mabon instead of them. "Perhaps."

"That doesn't mean you can't see, though, right?" Goronwy said. "We won't be able to find the Treasures if you can't guide us."

Taliesin closed his eyes, and such was the bard's power that Goronwy could almost sense the threads of his sight leading out from this moment. Taliesin shook his head. "I can, and I can't. I fear now that my visions have played me false. Perhaps they were meant to because a greater power is influencing my gift—one with ends of his own that I don't share."

"This isn't the first time you've mentioned a greater power," Catrin said. "Who is it?"

"I cannot say just yet."

"Can't or won't?" she said.

Goronwy found his hand going to the small of Catrin's back, and he turned her away from Mabon so they were huddled close to the bard, in the hope that Mabon couldn't overhear. "We should turn around now. We can't do our task with Mabon at our side. The best course of action I can think of is to return to Dinas Bran until this blows over and lock Mabon in the cellar where he can't do any harm."

"No." Catrin shook her head. "Who's to say what kind of damage he could do even behind iron bars? A whisper in this guard's ear or a touch to that maid's hand, and he would spread his influence throughout the castle. He could bring down Cade's rule without even leaving his cell. Besides—" she shuddered, "—Dinas Bran isn't safe."

Goronwy frowned. It was in his mind that on the battlements Catrin had come to tell him about her fears, but like an idiot he hadn't paid heed to her at the time. "I'm also concerned about what Arianrhod hasn't told us. In particular, how long are we to put up with Mabon? You've said yourself, Taliesin, that a day in our world can be a week in theirs or vice versa. Perhaps our best option is to stay away from Dinas Bran but also not to seek the Treasures. That would prevent Mabon from seeking them too."

"We can't abandon our quest," Catrin said. "The Treasures—"

"Forget the Treasures! Who gives a damn about the bloody Treasures? I certainly don't. They're trinkets meant to drive men mad—nothing more or less."

Catrin studied Goronwy, seemingly unalarmed by his sudden anger, which was gone within a few heartbeats of its appearance anyway. He didn't know what it was about the girl, but she tugged on him. Some men might complain that Catrin made them uncomfortable, but except at the very first, Goronwy had never felt that way about her. They'd been thrown together often since they'd come north from Caerleon, and in all that time he'd never heard her babble, as some women did, or demand attention or conversation. She had the admirable talent of silence.

He put out a hand to her. "I'm sorry. I shouldn't have shouted, but Mabon is a *sidhe*. A few days, a few years—they are nothing to him."

Meanwhile, Taliesin's expression was as grave as Goronwy had ever seen it—and it had been plenty grave beneath the caverns of Caer Dathyl.

"I know you seek the Treasures," Mabon said loudly, finally having grown tired of being excluded. "Truly, I mean you no ill, and I can help you in your quest."

Goronwy eyed Mabon sourly. "Like you helped find them before the battle at Caer Fawr? We don't need that kind of help."

Mabon looked affronted. "I wasn't collecting them for myself!"

Catrin pounced on the admission. "If not for yourself, then for whom?"

At the question, Mabon seemed to realize that he'd given them new information because a sly look overcame his face. "That is not your concern." He turned away and began to saunter down the road, plucking daisies and throwing them onto the road as he did so. It was wanton destruction and typical of Mabon.

Taliesin watched Mabon's retreating back for a moment, and then he turned to Catrin and Goronwy. "Do you feel magic from him?"

Goronwy was already halfway into shaking his head before he realized that Taliesin hadn't been talking to him. He looked away, trying to appear as unconcerned as possible, as if it hadn't been strange at all that he had answered.

But Catrin had noticed, and she pinned him with her gaze.

Goronwy shifted uncomfortably. "What?"

"You know what," Taliesin said, proving not only that he'd been paying attention all along, but that Goronwy hadn't fooled him for a single day.

One of the things it was important to remember about Taliesin was that sometimes he was oblivious to everything that most men found interesting—wine, women, material possessions—such that a man forgot about the mind that lay beneath the vacant looks and absent-minded ramblings. Taliesin was a force to be reckoned with once he focused his attention on what he'd decided was important. Goronwy should have known that this day would come.

"What are we talking about?" Catrin looked from one man to the other.

Taliesin tsked through his teeth. "You would have heard of Goronwy's mother. Her name was Nest."

"The great seeress!" Catrin spun on her heel to face Goronwy. "When were you going to mention that you have the sight too?"

Goronwy cursed himself for letting down his guard and Mabon for distracting him. "Never." He just managed not to shrink away from her glare. "Let's just say that my abilities in that area are of far less consequence than yours."

Catrin's eyes flashed again, and she took a step towards him. "I knew from the first that there was something different about you, but you so steadfastly hid your gift that I kept telling myself I was mistaken. I wasn't!"

"No." Taliesin hummed a little tune under his breath.

Goronwy would find no help from that quarter, so he tried again to explain to Catrin. "I know so little—"

"That would be because you push your gift away and refuse to use what has been given to you. You should be ashamed of yourself." She huffed away from him, but then pulled up at the sight of Mabon, who had stopped his carnage among the flowers and was watching their exchange with blatant curiosity.

None of them thought it was a good idea to show weakness or disunity in front of him. So, under the watching eyes of Taliesin, Goronwy closed his eyes and quested into the depths of his soul for the power that lay dormant in the center of his being. He knew it was still there, even after all these years. All he had to do to awaken it was open the box where he'd hidden it.

Except it wasn't quite that easy. Even as he moved towards it in his mind and felt a flicker of power, he shied away—not so much at the light or heat, but at the uncomfortable feeling it gave him, like ants running up and down his arms. He recoiled and opened his eyes.

"It's still there," Catrin said, in what he sensed was meant to be a reassuring manner. "You just need practice."

Mabon guffawed. "I could have told you that."

Goronwy reached for Catrin's hand and spoke in an undertone meant only for Catrin's ears. "But would he have?"

Her mouth twitched, which was what he'd hoped for.

"You're not forgiven," she said.

"I should hope not." Goronwy smiled to himself. Amusement was better than fear or anger, and if any of them were going to survive the next few days, they would need to keep their wits about them. "You are not wrong. I shouldn't have let my gift go unused all these years."

She canted her head. "Then again, perhaps you didn't. Aren't your abilities on the battlefield in part because you can sense a warrior's movements before he makes them?"

It was what Goronwy himself had thought. He cleared his throat, realizing as he did so that he should never disparage his gifts again in front of her. He wondered if Cade knew too and decided immediately that if he hadn't fooled Taliesin, he hadn't fooled Cade either. Then Catrin squeezed his hand to show that maybe she really had forgiven him. The sight of her upturned nose and the splash of freckles across her cheeks left him momentarily nonplussed.

To mask his confusion, he took a few quick steps to move slightly in front of her so she couldn't see his face—though he continued holding her hand. Silently, Goronwy and Catrin followed Taliesin, filing past Mabon who stood in the middle of the road, not moving. For all that he had wanted to carry on earlier, now he was unhappy. Perhaps Goronwy's jibes had gotten to him after all. Goronwy didn't look back, but after they'd gone a dozen yards he wasn't surprised to hear Mabon's crunching footsteps on the road behind them. Then Mabon came abreast, swinging his arms, the supercilious expression returned to his face. "I don't need looking after."

"Good," Goronwy said. "Because I have no intention of looking after you."

Mabon quickened his pace in order to pass Goronwy and Catrin and catch up with Taliesin. "I could go my own way, and you would have to come with me."

"I would have to do no such thing." Taliesin's legs were long, and Mabon skipped once to stay on pace.

"Where are we going? You must tell me."

Taliesin continued walking, making Mabon wait for an answer or, more likely, lost in his own thoughts and only remembering after some time had passed that Mabon had wanted something more from him. "We are going to the abbey."

That they finally had a destination was welcome news to Goronwy, but Mabon recoiled. "Which—which abbey?"

Taliesin gestured ahead. They had come the last few paces down the mountain. "Valle Crucis Abbey, which lies along this path northwest of the castle."

"Why would you go there?" Mabon said.

"To find answers."

"What answers?" Mabon said.

"If we knew the answers, we would hardly need to go there to find them, would we?" Goronwy said.

Mabon swung around to glare at Goronwy. "I have a right to know—"

Goronwy overrode him. "When you are ready to tell us what you're really doing here, we will let you in on what we're doing here. Until then, you can cease to speak."

Likely, nobody had ever spoken to Mabon this way in the eternity of his existence. The *sidhe* clenched his hands into fists and stepped in front of Goronwy. "How dare you—" But instead of finishing his sentence, he swung with his right fist at Goronwy in a roundhouse motion Goronwy saw coming before the thought of hitting him had formed completely in Mabon's mind.

Although Goronwy had many weapons at his disposal, he didn't need any of them. He merely sidestepped Mabon's punch, such that Mabon, who'd expected to connect with Goronwy's face, lost his balance on the follow through, spun, flailed, and then, having reached the edge of the road where it ended in a downward slope, lost his balance. He shrieked in a satisfyingly ungodlike fashion and fell.

Catrin edged closer to Goronwy as they looked over the edge of the road at Mabon. "He will hate you forever for this."

"He will, but how is that different from how he felt about me—and all of us—before today?"

Mabon growled as he clambered back up the slope. Despite his supposed lack of power, his clothes showed no evidence of dust, which meant his glamour was firmly in place. He glared at Goronwy, and then he transferred his gaze to Catrin. The god's lecherous smile made Catrin look down at her feet, and Goronwy wanted to punch him for real this time.

But instead, he took Catrin's elbow and set off with her down the road towards the abbey. Meanwhile, the awful truth resonated through his whole being, and he didn't need to tap into his sight to see it: controlling Mabon in human form might prove to be even more difficult than controlling him as a *sidhe*.

6

Catrin

"How far to the abbey from here?" Mabon hustled to catch up with them instead of affecting his usual arrogant saunter.

"Eight miles," Catrin said.

Mabon was silent for a moment. And then, "Did you say eight?"

Catrin didn't answer. Neither did the men, though Catrin caught the twitch at the corner of Goronwy's mouth. He would have complained about the distance if Mabon hadn't been with them—and he knew it. Taliesin, of course, didn't usually answer any questions or say anything at all. He'd spoken more in the last hour than Catrin had heard from him ever. Sometimes Taliesin's silence was an aggravating trait, but in this case, he was right not to answer. Mabon had heard Catrin fine the first time.

"What's wrong with riding horses?" Mabon planted himself in the middle of the road and spoke in a loud voice—

loud enough to wake the peasants in the house across a pasture from the road.

It was Goronwy who answered. "Taliesin likes to feel the earth beneath his feet."

Mabon snorted at that—a remarkably similar sound to the one Goronwy had made in response to the same information. This time Goronwy defended Taliesin, which was equally amusing in its way. "Taliesin says that where we're going, horses would be a hindrance."

Mabon stared at the back of Taliesin's head while the bard marched steadfastly on, ignoring them. Catrin had come to understand that it wasn't that he was absentminded. It was rather that he was listening to so many different voices—in his head, from the earth, from the *sidhe*—that it took all his focus and energy to keep them distinct. Speaking to an actual, living person was a fourth voice that at times was beyond his abilities.

For her part, as Catrin started walking again, avoiding the rain-filled ruts made by centuries of cart wheels, she felt connected to the earth for the first time in weeks. She tested the currents in the air and breathed deeply. Neither the unrest within Mabon nor her uncertainty about journeying with Goronwy once again, could dismay her. When she'd arrived at the gate and seen Taliesin leaving, she'd known that it was her role to go with him. It hadn't been in any way part of her plan—and quite the opposite, in fact—to find Goronwy alongside her too.

"You mean the world of the *sidhe*." Mabon hurried to pass Taliesin and then turned around to come to a halt in front of him, forcing Taliesin to choose between stopping or going around him.

Taliesin stopped.

"How are you going to get there? My mother said—"

Taliesin sighed. "I know what your mother said, but Beli's restrictions apply to you, not me. A path that should still be open lies beneath the abbey, which is why we're going there." He looked Mabon up and down. "As I said."

Taliesin actually hadn't said anything before about a path to the Otherworld underneath the abbey. Catrin was sure of it. Still, she could see now why horses might prove a hindrance, even if a three-hour walk in the middle of the night meant no sleep for any of them. Maybe Taliesin didn't need to sleep at all. Catrin didn't know the bard well enough to judge.

Mabon's eyes were still narrowed at Taliesin. His earlier amusement had vanished as quickly as it had come. If they were going to survive, they would all need to get used to these abrupt mood swings and figure out how to manage them. Mabon pointed with his chin at Catrin, who was standing just beyond Taliesin's left shoulder. "I wouldn't have brought a woman on this adventure, but I can see why you couldn't resist, old boy." He clapped a hand on the Taliesin's shoulder. "She provides good sport, does she?"

Catrin was so shocked, she laughed. Taliesin stared at Mabon blankly, and Catrin laughed again because she wasn't sure that Taliesin realized what Mabon had just suggested. Goronwy, on the other hand, moved so quickly that, before Mabon could see him coming, he had Mabon's feet pulled out from under him with a sweep of a leg. Mabon sprawled on his back on the ground, with the tip of Goronwy's sword to his throat. If Mabon had still been a *sidhe*, he could have slowed time and deflected Goronwy, but he'd lost the ability for now.

Despite her appreciation of his actions and skill, Catrin put her hand on Goronwy's free arm. "Don't kill him."

"I don't care who your mother is." Goronwy glared down at Mabon. "You will never speak of Catrin that way again."

Mabon put up his hands, palms out. His eyes were so wide it looked as if he was trying to see under his chin to determine how close the sword was to breaking the skin. "I didn't mean anything by it."

"You most certainly did," Goronwy said.

Catrin glanced at Taliesin, who was gazing north and not speaking—not even paying attention as far as Catrin could tell. The man truly was a mystery. She turned back to Goronwy. "Let him go, my lord. He isn't worth whatever trouble killing him would cause."

"It would be worth it," Goronwy said, but he stepped back and sheathed his sword. "He calls himself a god, but he isn't worthy to polish your boots." He spat on the ground beside Mabon.

Mabon scrambled to his feet and scuttled away, putting Taliesin between him and Goronwy.

"Apologize to Catrin." Taliesin still hadn't looked at any of them, but his words proved he'd been listening all along.

Mabon's mouth worked. At first Catrin thought he was going to refuse, but then he straightened and bowed in Catrin's general direction. "I apologize, Madam. I meant no disrespect." With an abrupt turn, he faced north and set off walking. A moment later, Taliesin was marching along after him.

From beside Catrin, Goronwy growled something barely intelligible, but included profanity and a comment about Mabon's antecedents.

"You shouldn't say such things, even if Arianrhod and Arawn aren't listening." Catrin still had a hand on his arm, and she squeezed it once, gently, before letting go. "Thank you. No one has ever defended my honor before."

Goronwy growled again. "That almost makes it worse. It was an honor to defend you."

Ahead of them, Mabon's mouth remained closed and his shoulders hunched, momentarily subdued by what had happened.

Goronwy aside, it was good to have more proof, before they traveled any farther on this journey, that Mabon was a mortal man as Arianrhod had promised. Goronwy could have killed him. Catrin almost regretted that she'd intervened.

Catrin eyed the god as he stalked a few paces away. Once they resumed walking, he kept his distance from them all, to the point that it seemed at times that he was leading their party down the road instead of Taliesin. Certainly he was actively avoiding Goronwy. Another few paces, and they had reached another house. A baby cried inside, and his mother hushed him. Catrin didn't think she was mistaken that she heard a hint of fear in the mother's voice.

Goronwy poked his head through the doorway, which was covered by a leather curtain, and spoke softly enough that Catrin couldn't hear him. Then he backed away as a young man—perhaps only a year or two into his manhood—stepped out.

"You have need of me, my lord?"

"I have a message for you to deliver to the castle," Goronwy said.

"At this hour? The woods are full of demons!"

"Don't pretend to me that you care. You aren't afraid of the dark; anyway, you were getting up within the hour to visit your girl in the village."

The boy's expression turned sheepish. "It's a long way up to the castle though, and she's waiting for me."

"It'll be faster if you run." And then Goronwy gave him a summary of what had happened since they'd left the castle, leaving nothing out, including Mabon's recent encounter with the Goronwy's sword.

The young man stared at him, his eyes as big as trenchers. Goronwy lifted his chin to point in the direction of the castle. "Go."

The young man ducked his head in a quick bow. "Yes, my lord. It is done." He ran off.

"You gave him an earful. That's a great deal to remember," Catrin said as she watched the boy's retreating back.

"He will remember it. He has a bard's gift for it."

"Our visit here will be all over the countryside tomorrow."

"The boy can keep a secret too. It would be best if the news that spreads is no more exciting than that we passed through. As long as the *sidhe* walk among us, it could be very much worse than that."

7

Taliesin

It was well past midnight when the companions reached Valle Crucis: the Valley of the Cross. It was a peaceful spot, with green fields and a brook running merrily through the grounds.

"The Horn of Immortality isn't here you know, if that's why we've come," Mabon said as they halted in front of the gatehouse. "I already looked."

Goronwy edged between Taliesin and Mabon. "When was this?"

Since the time of the Romans, the abbey had been a place of pilgrimage for Christians, not only throughout Britain, but in other countries as well. It was here that men believed Joseph of Arimathea had left the Cup of Christ. The pilgrims were right, of course, but Taliesin was pleased that the secret of the horn's location remained his and Cade's. Though he was surprised too, since the darkness beneath

Dinas Bran shouldn't have been difficult to detect. And yet, Arianrhod had not mentioned it.

Mabon shrugged. "Months ago now." He grinned at Taliesin. "Don't worry, the monks won't know me in this guise. I'm looking forward to hearing what they have to say when you ask for it."

Taliesin thought but didn't say, "Who says I'm here to ask for it?" Instead he gave way to Catrin, who said, "What did they tell you?"

"Nothing of use," Mabon said.

"You didn't hurt any of them, did you?" Catrin said.

"Of course not." And then Mabon laughed—one that sent shivers down Taliesin's spine. "Not in a way that any of them would remember."

Goronwy put his hand on the hilt of his sword, but then eased it away before leaning in to whisper to Taliesin. "I can't tell if he's telling the truth, or if he speaks as he does merely to aggravate."

Taliesin's gifts hadn't deserted him in this instance, because he himself could tell. "A little of both. Remember, he's been walking among humans for countless years. He knows something of us."

"Our weaknesses, surely," Goronwy said. "He has seemed continually surprised, however, that we have strengths too."

And that was definitely one of Mabon's weaknesses. With a nod from Taliesin, Goronwy pulled a rope, and a bell chimed inside the abbey, though not with a tolling sound as when a church called people to worship, but with just a little tinkling somewhere close by.

While Catrin waited patiently, as was her fashion, Goronwy stood with his arms folded across his chest and stared impassively at the door. Mabon shifted from foot to foot, already bored. Taliesin himself kept his eyes on the gatekeeper only he could see: a wizened old monk who crouched by the door, smiling at one and all. Taliesin nodded at him, and the man smiled back.

It couldn't quite be said that Taliesin could see ghosts, since ghosts didn't exist as most people thought of them. They could not harm or affect normal men. What did exist was a spiritual remnant of the dead, which remained behind in the same way that their physical remains could still be seen. Nobody occupied these misty beings most of the time, but an occasional soul had the wherewithal to return to this plane of existence by animating their spiritual form. Such a creature couldn't harm the living, but he could speak to them.

Or, at least, he could speak to Taliesin. Taliesin's sight may have failed far too many times this evening, but he had other gifts to call upon. This ghost might not know what lay beneath the abbey, but there were others in the abbey who did. While Taliesin didn't have a choice but to follow the path that lay before his feet, he would keep an eye out for any shade who could speak to him about the dangers he faced.

Finally, footsteps could be heard on the other side of the door, and a window in it opened.

"Who wakes us at this hour?" A man with white whiskers stuck his pointed nose through the opening. Taliesin didn't answer, just looked at him. The man pursed his lips, clearly not happy about Taliesin's presence, but he nodded anyway. "Right."

The door opened, and the man gestured to the companions that they should enter. With a last glance at the spirit at the door, who was still chuckling to himself, Taliesin led the way inside.

But not everyone was able to follow. As Catrin made to cross the threshold behind Taliesin, the gatekeeper's arm swung up to block her. "We do not suffer women to enter our presence."

While Taliesin had been speaking to him, Catrin had been standing to the right of Goronwy, hidden by his bulk, so the gatekeeper hadn't seen her at first.

It wasn't as if Taliesin had forgotten that the monks here didn't like women, but he had no patience with such prejudice either. Women were a focus of spiritual energy and were more emotional and intuitive than men by nature. These monks were fools to exclude them from their practices.

"Why not?" Mabon's chin stuck out in a look that had become very familiar.

"Evil resides within them," the monk said.

Taliesin rubbed his chin, feeling the bristles just poking through the skin. He hadn't shaved this morning. "She is with me."

"It does not matter. It is our law."

Mabon suddenly grinned. "You are more foolish than I expected if that's what you think women are about."

For the first time ever, Taliesin agreed with Mabon. That wouldn't do at all. But at the same time, he would not side with the monks. Any man who could dismiss his own mother as a source of evil had no place in Taliesin's world. Fortunately, these monks were an isolated sect, and their beliefs were shared by no other abbey in Wales that Taliesin knew of—or he would have been speaking more pointedly to Cade about the proclivities of this god of his.

Catrin shot Mabon a sour look. "It's all right, Taliesin. Maybe this wasn't a good idea after all."

Goronwy wasn't having any of it. "I have been baptized, and I have never heard of such a prohibition." He shouldered his way forward, elbowing the monk in the chest as he crossed the threshold. The man fell back. Since Goronwy's arm was around Catrin's waist, she came with him whether the monk liked it or not. Then Goronwy pulled the hood of Catrin's cloak over her head to hide her hair. "We won't be but a moment."

"N-n-n-no, please, my lord." The monk was stuttering, shocked to find himself disobeyed. "I cannot allow it! My abbot will punish me—"

"Then don't tell him." Goronwy looked at Taliesin. "We should be about whatever business you have here."

Ignoring the monk's fluttering anxiety, Taliesin marched across the courtyard and straight up to the great double doors of the main church building. Matins, the midnight vigil, had come and gone, and there was nobody else around. Mabon, Goronwy, and Catrin followed, along with the monk, who was still protesting.

Taliesin stopped on the threshold and allowed the others to pass him. Rather than leave the peacemaking entirely to Goronwy, which might be amusing, he spread his arms wide and filled the doorway, preventing the monk from entering the church after them. "We have business that does not include you. Return to the gatehouse and forget that we were ever here." It was the voice of Command, one Taliesin did not often use, and barely used in this case, putting only a little force into his words. He'd known in advance that the gatekeeper was suggestible. As he'd told the others, he'd been here before.

The monk's eyes glazed for a heartbeat and then cleared. When they did, he was no longer looking at Taliesin. A scuff mark on the frame of the door had caught his eye, and he licked his finger and rubbed at it. Then he turned away, muttering about careless novices.

Goronwy stepped to Taliesin's side and watched the monk walk back across the courtyard. "Do I want to know what you did to him?"

"I gave him a slight nudge in the direction he wanted to go. He didn't want to wake the abbot and wanted this problem to simply go away—so I encouraged him to think that it had. He is much happier now." Taliesin closed the door with a gentle thud.

If Taliesin had been alone, he might have opened and closed the door again, just to appreciate how well made it was and how easily the heavy door swung. Catrin gained her strength, as did most seeresses, from the living creatures that filled the earth. Taliesin, on the other hand, drew his power from the earth itself—from soil and stone. Many druids made a wood or forest their center of worship, but it was equally likely to find them in stone circles and caves. Or it had been until the Romans came and murdered every druid they could find.

Catrin shook her head. "And some men question why I have not found the Church to be a haven for me."

"Taliesin took care of it." Goronwy took her arm. "Come on."

"Where are we going now?" Mabon headed down the nave.

"Taliesin?" Catrin glanced back.

"The crypt," Taliesin said.

"This way." Goronwy strode towards the altar, which lay in the exact center of the church, and then through the monks' choir, where they sat during their services. The steps to the crypt lay at their feet.

Taliesin meant to follow them, but instead he found his feet frozen to the ground at the sight of so many shades inside the church. Most were floating near the walls, paying no attention to their surroundings, but four or five turned to look at Taliesin. One wore the uniform of a Roman legionnaire, his helmet tucked under his arm. Another was dressed in ragged robes, and Taliesin recognized him as a fellow druid, though not one he knew personally.

"Blessings, friends," Taliesin said, though he didn't say the words out loud. He didn't need to.

The druid's eyes were full of concern. "Have you drunk from the holy well?"

"I have," Taliesin said.

The druid nodded. "Then you may enter. But beware. All is not as it seems."

"If I know anything, I know that."

The druid glided closer, his eyes focused intently on Taliesin. "You are not like the others." He looked him up and down. "I am forbidden to say more. Know only that the one you fear is close, and he seeks you too."

Taliesin assumed the shade meant Efnysien, but whether he was right didn't seem like a question he could ask. "I seek nothing for myself."

"So we understand. That is the only reason you have been permitted to continue." The ghost faded backwards, towards the legionnaire, and his last words echoed in

Taliesin's ear. "You are a rare one, Taliesin, and more important than you know."

Taliesin found himself shaking a little as he approached the stair. Mabon had picked up a candle from the monks' altar and was waiting for Taliesin with it. Though Taliesin had been to the church before and for years had wanted to descend into the crypt, he'd never done so. Perhaps that was just as well, since from what the ghost had said, he might not have been given admittance.

The abbey had been built over the top of an ancient cave in which his people had worshipped before the Romans had come to their land. Inside Taliesin, a chorus rose up as the men who'd come before him worried about what damage the monks might have done to their sacred site. He told them to hush and that they would soon find out.

This adopting and coopting of ancient holy sites had been happening since the first priests came to Britain, as Christians attempted to convince the people that worshipping the Christ was only a step from worshipping the old gods. It meant that tunnels, whether built by the ancients, Romans, or early Christians, were found at virtually every church and fort throughout Britain. In many cases, the secrets that lay beneath had been forgotten or destroyed but, as at Dinas Bran, the core of what had once been a holy site to someone remained.

Taliesin resented the way this new religion appropriated the symbols of the old for its own purposes, but he told himself to be pleased too, for their actions meant the Christian monks hadn't destroyed the cave, as they could have. It was to this cave, in fact, that Joseph of Arimathea had first brought the Cup of Christ for safekeeping, knowing that nobody would look for it among pagan artifacts. When he died, he'd been buried beneath the mountain upon which the castle of Dinas Bran rested—also above a sacred druidic site and entry point to the Otherworld—and the Cup with him.

Until Cade and Taliesin had permanently buried Joseph and his Cup inside the mountain, Taliesin hadn't connected the Cup of Christ to the horn recorded in his own tradition as a great Treasure. But he was beginning to understand that the connection was not limited to the cup.

He wasn't a Christian, but he'd learned their myths out of self-preservation. If the Cup of Christ was the same Horn of Immortality of druidic legend, then other artifacts could have a similar counterpart. For example, it might be that the Mantle was made from the cloth in which Christ's body had been wrapped; the knife, which had also been found, was the weapon that had pierced Christ's side as he hung on the cross at Calvary; even Dyrnwyn was the sword of fire held by the angel of heaven who guarded the entrance to the Garden of Eden. And so on.

Goronwy looked at Taliesin over the top of Catrin's head. "It's really dark down there."

Taliesin studied the unlit steps. "I fear it too."

When the others looked at him anxiously, Taliesin blinked, realizing that he'd spoken those last words out loud. As at Dinas Bran, Taliesin felt the dark force beneath his feet, thrumming to get out. "I fear that you may regret coming with me."

Goronwy had one hand on the hilt of his sword and held Catrin's hand in the other. "That may be, but we're coming anyway."

Taliesin put out a hand, blocking the descent of the others and said, "I will go first."

With a blink of his eye, he lit the end of his staff again, and the little light illumined a few feet of space in front of him. He started down the steps, followed by Mabon, and then Goronwy and Catrin. The door into the crypt was easily pushed open, and a long tunnel stretched before them.

"Does it—does it have an ending?" Catrin said.

Taliesin didn't bother answering, because she wouldn't like his reply: *It does, and it doesn't.*

Goronwy pulled his sword from its sheath. "I don't like this at all."

"You aren't meant to," Taliesin said.

8

Rhiann

Rhiann arrived in the courtyard, her recent conversation with Cade ringing in her ears.

"With all that has happened, I'm still riding to Caer Fawr with you tonight? Why?"

Cade had given her a quizzical look. "Don't you want to? Are you tired of my company already?"

Rhiann made a face. "Don't be silly. Of course I want to come with you. I'm just surprised that you think it's a good idea. It would be much more likely for you to want to send me somewhere else where I'll be safe."

"I would be more of a fool than I actually am to think that any of us are safe anywhere else," Cade said. "Even with the sidhe cutting themselves off from our world, we have plenty of mortal enemies—and who's to say that Mabon is the only sidhe who walks among us?"

"Do you believe Mabon when he says he means us no ill?"

"I believe that—up to a point and only as far as it gives him rope to hang himself."

Peada had already departed with his men, having eaten the evening meal in double time. Rhiann had climbed to the battlement to watch them pound down the road, ultimately turning northeast towards Chester, which was where he said he was going. Rhiann had never been to Chester. Before leaving Anglesey with Cade, she'd barely ever left Aberffraw, much less visited England. If she'd married Peada as her father had wanted, she might have ended up there anyway, even if she would have been a different person inside.

At Rhiann's entrance, Angharad lifted her bag to show Rhiann that she'd brought it. "We've been settled for two months, but I've been ready for days to leave at a moment's notice." She lifted her chin to point to the crowded courtyard. It was the same organized chaos that always accompanied a departure from the castle. "Where are the others?"

"Goronwy and Catrin went off with Taliesin, and Hywel and Bedwyr are following Peada to Chester. If all goes well, they will ride afterwards to Caer Fawr. But Taliesin wanted us to leave, so we'll head south tonight. The other lords will be gathering too." Rhiann shivered slightly. "It feels all of a sudden as if we've sat on this mountaintop too long."

Dafydd appeared in the doorway behind Rhiann. "It's time."

Angharad looked up at her husband. "How far is it to Chester?" She had never been to England either.

"Some twenty miles, a little more," Dafydd said. "Hywel and Bedwyr will have no trouble."

"We've ridden less far in more peril." Rhiann shook her head. "Taliesin's fears have spilled over to me. I can't help feeling as if the danger we face is worse than anything we've seen so far."

"Worse!" Angharad's emerald eyes flashed. "I hope not. At least Penda is human."

"Humans can be more inventive in their cruelty than the *sidhe*," Rhiann pointed out.

Dafydd held out his hand to Angharad, and she took it. The pair had married within a few weeks of their victory at Caer Fawr. Some might have said they'd married in haste, but their friends agreed with them that life was too short to dawdle.

Cade was riding with nearly the full complement of men he kept at Dinas Bran. He'd sent home most of the men who'd fought at Caer Fawr, knowing they needed to see to the spring planting and newborn lambs, but he kept a contingent of forty knights with him at all times and would leave only ten to garrison Dinas Bran.

Rhiann walked up to her husband and put a hand on his arm. "What's wrong?"

Cade had been gazing pensively towards the keep. At her question, he blinked and looked down at her. "I'm trying to see the future."

Despite the tension in the air, or maybe because of it, she laughed. "Taliesin couldn't tell us exactly what is to come. Why do you think you should be able to?"

"It is a king's duty to head off trouble before it starts." He frowned. "I sent all of my seers off with Taliesin, and perhaps I shouldn't have done that."

Rhiann looked at him quizzically. "All your seers? You mean Catrin?"

"Goronwy is one too." He gave a quick shake of his head. "I'm sorry I never told you, but he avoided speaking of it to anyone."

Rhiann let out a breath of surprise. "I never even guessed."

"I fear the trouble they might find on this path Taliesin has chosen."

"The trouble started long before you were born. We may keep it at bay for a time, but we can only do the best we can with what we have been given."

He smiled at her. "Accept what is before me and what I cannot change, is that it?" He gently boosted Rhiann onto her horse. She was still early enough into her pregnancy that it hardly showed, but they were both always conscious of the other heart beating inside her and their need to protect it.

"You said it, not me. I only meant that you didn't create the problems before us. You inherited them." Then Rhiann felt a gust of air on her cheek and turned into it. The weather rarely came from the north, especially at this time of year and at this hour of the night. Cade noted her concern and asked about it.

"I was just thinking that it's an odd time for the wind to change direction."

"Nothing about tonight feels as it should. Taliesin was right. We should get moving." His hand on the hilt of his sword, as if the weapon would help against the storm that was coming, Cade ran to his own horse and mounted.

Dafydd was acting as Cade's captain tonight, and all Cade's men required was a jerk of Dafydd's head to know that it was time to go. As they rode under the gatehouse, Cade tucked his horse in close to Rhiann's, the pair of them third in the line of horses.

As they left the castle behind them, Rhiann gripped the reins tightly with both hands. "Something is wrong, Cade. Even I can feel it." They were moving at a canter, which was a little fast for the terrain, but their speed brought them a third of the way down the mountain in a matter of a quarter-hour.

Cade reached out a hand and briefly squeezed her shoulder. "I know how you feel, but I don't know what's wrong—and believe me, I don't like that I don't know."

Boom!

Every horse in the company staggered, and then the lead horse reared. The rider, Gruffydd, struggled for control even as he loosened his feet in the stirrups in preparation for jumping off. The horse didn't give him the chance, however, and a heartbeat later, it took off down the road at a gallop.

It was only as her own horse bucked that Rhiann realized that the ground, as well as her horse, was shaking. Her elbow bumped into Cade's as he leaned over to grasp her horse's bridle. "Follow Gruffydd! Ride now!"

Dafydd, who'd been keeping to a position just in front of Cade, Angharad at his side, relayed the order. As one, the company charged after the spooked horse. It was actually easier to urge her horse into a gallop than it had been for Rhiann to try to control it. As it raced down the mountain, the horse spent as much time in the air as on the ground and, once in motion, Rhiann hardly noticed the shifting earth beneath its feet.

They kept going until they were almost to the village, at which point the road narrowed at the river crossing, and they were forced to slow. Normally Rhiann's horse was as sedate as could be, but she continued to shake. The earth itself, however, had stopped. Cade ordered everyone to dismount on the near side of the bridge, and Rhiann and Angharad threw their arms around each other.

Angharad's mane of red curls had come loose from its bindings and formed a halo around her head. "Is this Mabon's doing?" She pressed down on her hair, trying to tame the loose strands.

Rhiann wanted to reassure her friend but couldn't find the words. "I don't know. I don't think anyone does."

But Angharad's attention had been drawn to the top of the mountain. Rhiann turned to look with her to where the castle loomed above them.

Or used to.

The familiar battlements had vanished, to be replaced by a pall of smoke that was visible against the risen moon and stars. Cade reached for Rhiann's hand, and as he held it, she realized that her skin was as cold as his. By then, everyone was looking up, and such was the discipline of Cade's men that nobody panicked, though a few scattered curses rebounded among them.

"We could have been inside that," Rhiann said, putting into words what many were thinking. She glanced at her husband. "Taliesin's prescience saved us."

"It was actually Catrin's," Cade said.

One of Cade's men, Aron, an older fellow with a thick, mostly gray beard approached. "What about those who remained behind? We should return to help them."

"I fear for them as much as you, Aron. But I can tell you right now that I cannot return to the mountain top. Can't you see that I, at least, am not wanted?"

"Cade—" Rhiann started to protest, but he spoke over her.

"It has become clear to me, if it wasn't already, that my task lies elsewhere. We will roust the village—those who aren't already awake—and send to the top of the mountain all who are able to help." He clapped a hand on Aron's shoulder. "Choose ten of our men to assist you."

Aron swallowed hard. "Yes, my lord. What about you? Will you still ride to Caer Fawr as you planned?"

"Caer Fawr holds no answers for me this night." Cade swung around to look north. Then he lifted his chin so his voice would carry to all the men. "We ride to Chester."

Dafydd's brows drew together, but he didn't argue. None of the men did, so it was left to Rhiann to ask what they were all thinking, though she spoke softly so only her husband could hear her. "Is that wise, Cade? We would be escaping one danger only to embroil ourselves in another."

Cade put his arm around her and pulled her close. "Earlier I spoke of Chester as the lion's den. Now I'm wondering if it wasn't Peada who walked into it instead. Perhaps I should be thanking the Mercians instead of cursing them."

Rhiann wrapped her arms around her husband's waist. "How could this happen? What made the mountain shake so?"

"I have spoken to you of the darkness there. I fear the *sidhe* are continuing to meddle in our affairs, regardless of what Arianrhod said to Taliesin."

Rhiann nodded. If it was the darkness that had awakened, the message it was sending was clear: don't come back.

9

Catrin

As the ground shook and shook, the hair on the back of Catrin's neck stood straight up, and the chill running down her spine wasn't just from the cold air that had pooled in the tunnel. She had hesitated so long in the doorway before starting after Taliesin that he and Mabon had gotten quite far ahead before she found the courage to put one foot in front of the other. Up ahead in the darkness, the sound of laughter came, cut off a moment later.

"That sounded like Mabon," Goronwy said.

As the shaking abated, Catrin picked up the pace, only barely keeping the light of Taliesin's staff in sight. She had stopped trying to pull her hand from Goronwy's, because it only made him hold on tighter. Back at Dinas Bran, she had meant to walk away from him, only to find him asking to come on the journey too. While on one hand, she had no interest in leaving his side, on the other, it was a constant ache to be with him—a kind of torture, even, made worse by the fact that she was doing it to herself.

And then as they came around a corner, they both stopped, a gasp forming in Catrin's throat, though the sound never reached her lips. Mabon and Taliesin stood before a doorway—or what seemed to be a doorway if doorways came four-feet wide, eight-feet tall, and ringed in purple light.

Mabon looked back at them. "What took you so long?"

Catrin stepped closer, and this time it was Goronwy who held back. By the time she realized how reluctant he was feeling, she was tugging him along. "Where does it lead to?"

"Nowhere good," Goronwy said.

"It leads to neither good nor evil, any more than the human world is good or evil. It leads to a place that *is*." Taliesin spoke straightforwardly, fully focused on what he was doing to create the doorway—or maybe simply to reveal it.

Mabon was practically bouncing up and down with excitement. "We're going home!"

"Have you ever gone this way before, Taliesin?" Goronwy said.

Taliesin turned to look at the knight, and there was something in his eyes that made Catrin want to take a step back, though she didn't since that would put her right into

Goronwy. "Not recently. Not from here." He tipped his head towards the door. "It's ready."

Mabon continued to gibber away, making chortling noises and rubbing his hands together in his excitement.

Catrin frowned at him. "Why are you so happy?"

"My family banished me to the human world, and here I am, going right back only a few hours later."

"You do realize that you're doing so as a human? That whatever you feel when you are there—whatever powers you have had in the past—you won't have now?" Goronwy said.

The corners of Mabon's mouth turned down, and he glared at Goronwy, though he didn't argue with his conclusion. What Goronwy said was true. Instead he turned to Taliesin. "Does he have to come?"

"He does." Taliesin grasped Goronwy's left elbow in one hand and Mabon's right with the other. Lifting his chin to point at Catrin, he said to Goronwy, "Hold on to her."

Catrin felt herself grasped around the waist as Goronwy pulled her to his side with his right arm and gripped her upper left arm with his left hand.

"All together now." Taliesin stuck out his left foot and held it in front of him.

It took a moment for Catrin to realize that he wanted everyone to step across the threshold at exactly the same moment. She put out her foot too and, after a brief sigh, so did Goronwy. Mabon, eyes alight, had no such trepidation and stuck out his foot as if he was a posed child's doll.

Then Taliesin said, "We'll step down on three ... one—two—"

They each dropped a left foot over the threshold at the same instant, squeezing through the doorway as they did so. Catrin didn't have to be warned by Taliesin that she didn't want the purple light coming anywhere near her right shoulder.

And then they were through as if the journey had been of no more consequence than entering the gatehouse of Dinas Bran. They all continued walking, still hanging on to each other and bunched together, which was all Catrin wanted to do anyway because she couldn't see anything at all. Immediately upon their entrance, the door disappeared, along with the purple light, to be replaced by a blackness so complete that Taliesin's little light showed her nothing at all.

She didn't know what she expected the Otherworld to look like—beautiful, certainly. She'd heard tales of Avalon where King Arthur, Cade's heroic ancestor, resided. She'd always imagined a land of silver and gold, like the sun shining through a very thin layer of mist, which might be swept to away to reveal the greens and blues of Wales in mid-summer.

"Where are we, Taliesin?" she whispered.

"We are between worlds," Mabon answered for him. His tone implied that this was exactly what he'd been expecting. Likely, it was, and even though it was Mabon who'd spoken, his serenity helped her to relax.

"Do you experience something like this each time you move between worlds?"

"Yes."

Catrin couldn't believe she was really having a conversation with Mabon, but it was he who'd answered, and he who had the answers. She still didn't trust him at all, but in this, she believed that he knew what he was doing, maybe more than Taliesin did.

Goronwy continued to keep her pressed close against his side and, for once, his sense of humor had deserted him. He gave her waist a quick squeeze—in moral support she thought—and they continued walking. And walking. Finally, he asked. "Are you sure this is right, Taliesin? We've come at least a mile."

"It only seems so." Like Mabon's, Taliesin's tone was perfectly calm, and again Catrin took comfort in another's certainty. "Almost there."

"Almost where?" Goronwy muttered in Catrin's ear, which drew a smile, as he meant it to.

And then the blackness was wiped away, like a blindfold suddenly pulled from a captive's eyes. Catrin stopped, shocked by the sudden brightness that assaulted her senses. She blinked and then blinked again, trying to master the stars that popped and sparkled across her vision.

Goronwy had stopped with her, and he put a hand to his eyes and bent his head. "Give it a moment."

Taliesin let go of Goronwy and Mabon and strode a few paces forward. When Catrin looked up, finally able to see, the bard was grinning from ear to ear. As Catrin's vision cleared, she saw why: the Otherworld *was* beautiful. And oddly familiar. She spun on one heel; the countryside was one she recognized. They had come out to the west of Valle Crucis Abbey.

Except the abbey was gone. They were standing on a grass-covered hill, but one without the sheep droppings that would normally have marred it. There were no stone walls, no fences—no human constructions of any kind except Dinas Bran, whose mountain she would have recognized in her sleep. She shielded her eyes against the sun in order to see it better, and was about to tell Goronwy to look with her, when she realized that it wasn't as they'd left it. At home, it was a bastion of Cade's power, but in this world, it was a ruin. Pieces of wall and tower stuck up here and there, but the majority of the castle had come down.

Beside her, Goronwy growled his dismay. He'd let go of her upper arm, but he hadn't taken his right arm from her waist, and now Catrin's hand went to where his hand rested. She gripped it for a moment and, though he hesitated initially, after a heartbeat he interlaced his fingers with hers.

They both turned at the same time to speak of their concerns to Taliesin, but he was looking the other way and face-to-face with Mabon.

"What have you done? Why are we *here?*" Mabon was apoplectic.

"What's wrong with here?" Taliesin said in that sunny way of his.

"It's—it's—" Mabon couldn't get the words out, rendered speechless by whatever atrocity Taliesin had subjected them to.

"It's where we needed to be. I'm sorry if you thought we were going to the High Court," Taliesin said. "Surely you must realize that I could not take these two on such a road?"

"Gah!" Sounding as human as any of them, Mabon spun around and stomped away. Unfortunately for him, the grass was wet—from dew or recent rain, though the day was bright and the sky cloud-free—and on his third stomp his foot slipped out from under him. With a squish, he fell on his rear, leaving a long, muddy skid in the grass.

Catrin looked away, deciding that laughter would be inappropriate.

Goronwy showed self-restraint too, though his desire to mock the child-god must have been nearly overwhelming. But then he frowned, and there was no humor in his voice at all. "Taliesin, tell us truly. Where are we?"

Leaving Mabon to get to his feet on his own, Taliesin turned to look at them. "Where do you think *here* is, Goronwy? The Otherworld is what you make it, didn't you know?"

Goronwy shook his head, hesitant for perhaps the first time in his life. "This is ... what the Otherworld looks like to you?"

"Not to me. This must be one of you, since that castle on the hill wasn't there the last time I was here. A reference point, I think."

Catrin looked past him to Mabon. "What about him?"

Taliesin turned, eyebrows raised. "He is very disappointed. He was expecting something different." He looked directly at Goronwy. "For Arthur, the Otherworld was a healing isle of peace and tranquility; for others, it is an endless Feast with bottomless pitchers of mead; for some, it is a fiery pit where they suffer for crimes that went unpunished in their mortal lives. The Otherworld becomes what those who pass into it need it—or imagine it—to be."

"A place of power," Goronwy said.

Taliesin snorted. "This is a place of power, as Mabon will soon discover." He cocked his head. "We won't tell him. Come." Then he set off at a brisk pace down the hill, heading west away from Dinas Bran.

Goronwy and Catrin hustled after him, and Catrin didn't even need to ask again where they were going, because they'd gone only a hundred yards before a castle—one of silver and gold like she'd imagined—appeared in the next valley where a moment before there'd been nothing but pastureland. The castle contained many doors and windows, but there was only one way into the keep from their current position, and that was through the front gate.

Behind them, Mabon laughed harshly. "You'd better know what you're doing, Taliesin, to venture in there."

Catrin had already started unthinkingly towards the castle, but at Mabon's laugh, she stopped. The castle was calling to her, like a bard playing a lyre, drawing her towards it. She shuddered and found herself agreeing yet again with Mabon.

A smile was playing around Taliesin's lips. "How quickly you forget that I didn't invite any of you to come."

10

Hywel

Ever since Caer Fawr, Hywel and Bedwyr had taken it upon themselves to act as scouts for Cade, even if to some men's eyes such duties were beneath knights. They didn't care what others thought—and, even more, they didn't trust anyone else to do as good a job.

"Cade and Dafydd should have sent Angharad and Rhiann away like I did Aderyn," Bedwyr said in an undertone, though his eyes never left the front line of the Northumbrian force that had appeared out of the pre-dawn gloom, advancing south upon Chester. He and Hywel were crouched behind a stone wall that marked the border of a field. Their intent had been to stay well away from the Northumbrian army, but Hywel was thinking now that they had to get closer.

He didn't mention that to Bedwyr yet, however, instead scoffing openly at Bedwyr's comment. Numerous marriages had occurred in the aftermath of Caer Fawr—out of a general sense of jubilation or because it had been impressed upon everyone that the time for such things was now or it could be never. Aderyn had been one of the healers who'd tended the men after the battle. "Your wife rode to help Bronwen at the birth of her child. It had nothing to do with your command."

Bedwyr grumbled under his breath, something about women knowing their own mind when they should be thinking of their husband's wishes, but he didn't mean it—any more than Cade might mean it if he'd been speaking of Rhiann. For Hywel's part, while he was pleased with the happiness in Bedwyr's face since he'd married, Caer Fawr had taught him quite the opposite lesson from everyone else: the last thing he wanted was to involve a woman in this life he was leading or bring a child into such a chaotic world.

"We need to warn the city," Hywel said.

Bedwyr shook his head. "Believe me. They already know. What Penda will need from us is their numbers and disposition."

"I don't relish the idea of entering a city about to be under siege."

"Nor I." Bedwyr shrugged. "Our orders are clear: to scout the situation, but to leave the fighting to Penda. His is a lost cause, and Cade wants us at Caer Fawr. I want to be at Caer Fawr."

For a moment the two men looked at each other, and then they nodded in unison, knowing that whatever they did, hurrying should be the first order of business. As one, they ran towards the woods to their right and then headed north, towards the Northumbrian army. The sun still hadn't risen, but it was coming. When they reached the next rise, they crouched at the top, and the light was enough to begin to make out the Northumbrians' numbers.

Bedwyr cursed under his breath. "This is only the leading edge."

Hywel pointed with his chin to a line of men carrying a ladder. "They know that Chester isn't defensible and don't intend a siege. They're going to go right over the walls."

"We need to get back before the sun rises, and we're caught," Bedwyr said.

They skirted the army to the east and ran to where they'd left their horses. They'd approached the Northumbrian lines from the southeast and now followed a parallel track to the path the Northumbrians were forging across the fields and pastures to the northeast of Chester. Once the track intersected the main road, they urged their horses into a gallop, heading for the eastern entrance to the city.

But as they turned onto the Roman road, before they crossed the last few hundred yards to the city, Bedwyr pointed southwest. "That's a sight that brings some cheer. Cade has come!"

Hywel shook his head in disbelief, even as he turned towards Gwynedd's banners. Cade's party was just crossing the bridge to the south of the city. "Cheering to us, but he said he wasn't coming. I fear what has caused him to change his mind."

"How is it that you're so gloomy all of a sudden? We've faced worse odds than this and won." Bedwyr directed his horse past the coliseum, along a minor road that would intersect with the south gate road. "After Cade's crowning, I'll be seeing about finding you a girl to bring a smile to your face."

Hywel growled back at his friend, but even so, he felt his spirits lift. How could they not at the sight of the dragon standard streaming in the wind ahead of them? When they reached the crossroads, they pulled up to wait for Cade's company, and the moment Cade was in earshot, Hywel said, "Northumbria comes."

"We knew they would." Cade reined in. "How many?"

"Two thousand," Bedwyr said flatly.

"Too many to feed for long." Cade's jaw clenched as he gazed northeast, though from this position, even if the sun had risen, the Northumbrian soldiers wouldn't yet be visible. The area around Chester as a whole was flat—far flatter than almost any region in Wales. That could be attributed in part to the winding of the River Dee. In fact, Chester's west gate was a water landing for boats with trade goods traveling south from the sea on the Dee.

Hywel nodded his assent. "Oswin isn't planning a siege."

Rhiann's attention had been drawn to the southern gatehouse where a dozen soldiers had gathered to look down upon them. "Taliesin is sure that Penda will die?"

"He is sure," Cade said, "though he was clear that it wouldn't be by Oswin's hand today."

Rhiann lifted her chin to indicate the city. "Will they have shelter for you?"

"I'm tempted to wear the mantle, just to confound my uncle and make him think I sent you without me, but that would be petty." Cade looked beyond the city to the eastern sky, which was lightening in advance of the dawn. Then he looked the other way and canted his head. "It won't matter soon if Penda does have shelter for me. Rain is coming."

Because of Cade's sensitivity to the sun, he was unusually attuned to the weather, though the storm clouds boiling on the western horizon would have been noticeable to everyone in another few moments.

"Perhaps Rhiann is right, my lord. We have no idea what we're getting into by riding in there." Dafydd took his station as one of Cade's captains very seriously.

"We don't," Cade agreed, "and I have no intention of staying. But my uncle and cousin are in there, along with all of their men, and even if they already know the size of the Northumbrian force, I might be the only one whose voice has the necessary weight to convince them to retreat."

"Retreat?" Hywel said.

"You're surprised?" Cade said. "You think I never saw a battle I didn't love?"

"I didn't say that," Hywel said.

"The survival of Wales isn't about pitched battles anymore. We're holding back the Saxon tide, but it will roll right over us if we don't choose our ground carefully, and this isn't the ground on which to make a stand." Cade looked around at his men. "We survived worse odds not long ago, I realize, but I think we need Penda to learn a Welsh lesson today."

Hywel let out a sharp breath. "To retreat to the hills, let the enemy take his city, and then when Oswin leaves, which he will, return and rebuild."

Cade gave Hywel an approving nod. "Oswin came to Chester to destroy Penda. He doesn't want to garrison the city."

"Why not?" Dafydd said.

"For the same reason I'm going to convince Penda to leave it. It isn't defensible," Cade said. "Trust me."

Hywel chewed on his lower lip. "We men are one thing, but I must point out that the women are safer outside than in."

"I don't know that any place is safe." And Cade told the two men about the fall of Dinas Bran.

Hywel stared at his king. "What is happening? Is it the end of the world?"

"Not the world," Cade said, "but maybe the end of our world as we know it."

11

Goronwy

"How do you want to handle this?" Goronwy said. "Straight up to the front door and knock like at Caer Ddu or go in the back way like at Caer Dathyl?"

Taliesin chewed on his lower lip as he studied the castle, uncharacteristically hesitant. "Which do you think turned out better?"

"Both have their merits. I think the straightforward approach is preferable to sneaking around, but this isn't my world, and I've never been here before."

"Neither have I," Taliesin said.

All three of Taliesin's companions gaped at him. "Then—then—" Catrin started to speak but immediately gave up.

"*I* have never been here before." As he spoke, Taliesin's voice deepened and grew scratchy, as if he'd spent too much time in a room full of thick smoke. "I didn't say that that I didn't know the way."

Goronwy felt a chill run through him. He didn't know very much about who or what the bard was, but from the few comments Cade and Taliesin himself had made about Taliesin's past, Goronwy had inferred that he'd lived many lives, as impossible as that sounded, as if his soul had been transferred from one body to another as soon as the physical shell had worn out.

It was an uncomfortable thought, though no different in principle from the idea that Cade was the return of King Arthur. Which was a known fact.

"I'm not going to ask what you know that we don't, Taliesin," Goronwy said, "because you'll only say *everything*, so instead I'll ask to whom that castle belongs."

Taliesin didn't respond immediately—and this time it wasn't as if he was lost in thought. Goronwy would have recognized that particular vacant expression if it were on Taliesin's face. Instead, it was as if he'd suddenly aged a hundred years. His back curved like an old man's, and his steps shortened.

Mabon was oblivious to the undercurrents and to Taliesin's physical transformation—or at least he was ignoring it. He kicked a rock out of the path and sneered,

"Caer Wydr belongs to my grandmother. I *cannot* believe you brought me here."

"Dôn isn't here just now," Taliesin said.

"I *know* that, but she could return at any moment!"

"I imagine she has other concerns—or at least I'm hoping she does," Taliesin said.

"You're *hoping*?" Goronwy said.

Taliesin canted his head, and for a heartbeat he was his young self again. "I have had no vision of this moment. It was one of the reasons I came. It seemed to me that something has been directing my *sight*—masking it, rather—and it was time to confront that power." Then he looked directly at Goronwy. "I would ask you to try again and *see*. Your abilities go beyond the strength of your arms. Catrin and I both sense the magic here, but you can see more than we can in this instance."

"How can you possibly think that?" Goronwy said.

Taliesin stepped closer and lowered his voice, so that his words were for Goronwy's ears alone. "I knew you as a boy, though you don't remember it. You can see auras, not only around people but around things. You can tell me if Mabon is who he says he is, and if this castle is where we need to be."

Goronwy wanted to shake his head and deny Taliesin's words, but instead he asked, "Why can't you?"

"There is a power here that is actively opposing me, but it doesn't know about you."

Goronwy groaned. "I don't—" He stopped as Taliesin continued to study him. "I don't know what you want. I walked away from anything that had to do with the world of the *sidhe* a long time ago."

"Try."

As if it had ever been that simple. But Goronwy could not say no to the bard. He closed his eyes as he had before and quested towards the source of power in the center of his being. The first time, he'd shied away, and he'd known he was doing it, even as he claimed that he'd tried.

But he hadn't really.

Taking in a deep breath, he imagined putting both hands on the lid of the box that contained his power and lifting it. As if it had been waiting for just this moment, the light at his center didn't hesitate. It blew off the lid in a glorious rush which had him seeing stars before his eyes, even with them closed.

"Goronwy?"

He felt Catrin's gentle hand on his arm, and he opened his eyes to find her gray ones assessing him. He was almost surprised that his surroundings looked exactly the same as they had a moment before, though he himself felt like he was on fire, with light bursting from his fingertips and from the top of his head. He wondered if, to Catrin and Taliesin, he looked a bit like Cade did when he allowed his power to show.

"Deep breath," she said.

He obeyed and felt the power receding to a more manageable level. He sensed more than outright saw the shimmer of gold surrounding Catrin. Taliesin's aura was deep indigo, of course, as befitting one with the third eye. Goronwy turned to Mabon, expecting to see him surrounded by black—and instead was surprised to see a healthier pinkish-red, admittedly somewhat muddied and combined with brown and orange. It had been nearly thirty years since Goronwy had allowed himself to see auras, but his mother had forced him to memorize the meanings of the colors, and those he would never forget. Mabon was angry, dishonest, and lazy, but he was also strong-willed and passionate.

Mabon glared back at Goronwy, no more contrite than he'd ever been. "You understand so little."

"He really does have no magic in him in this form," Goronwy said.

Mabon pouted and huffed like a five-year-old who'd just been told it was bedtime. "I could have told you that."

"What about the castle?" Taliesin said.

Goronwy wrenched his attention away from Mabon and looked where Taliesin pointed. Castles weren't people, though it was Goronwy's experience that buildings could take on something of the personality of their owner. To the naked eye, the castle was a silver shimmer in the sunlight. To Goronwy's inner eye, that silver was still there. Given that this was Dôn's home, an ingrained spiritual depth was to be expected. The aura was overlaid and diminished, however, by that blackness Goronwy had expected to see around Mabon. "Someone with a deep-seated hatred as well as grief is trying to capture Dôn's energy, even twist it to his own ends."

As the words left Goronwy's mouth, the wind picked up, and clouds began to skid across the sky. The temperature dropped precipitously. In another ten heartbeats, the companions were trembling from the cold—even Mabon, who cursed his human weakness and pulled his cloak closer around himself, and then the first flakes of snow began to fall.

"Someone defends," Mabon said, "but it isn't my grandmother's way to use cold."

"It could be Caillech," Catrin said. Caillech was the goddess of winter and servant of Dôn.

"No," Taliesin said, and then he added:

The mountain snows sweep over us
A knife sharpened to a thin edge
Cold indistinguishable from fear.

"Comforting," Goronwy said.

The others bent into the wind, which was blowing into their faces so hard that they could barely move, but they started forward anyway. Goronwy kept his head up, however, his eyes never leaving the tiers of ramparts and ditches that surrounded the castle, and somehow the storm wasn't affecting him like it was the others. Even as he wondered at what was happening to him, though preferring not to question it or his instincts, he pulled Catrin close to his side.

The moment her arm came around his waist, she stopped shivering, so he reached out a hand to Taliesin, who'd been forging ahead. As the bard came within the circle of Goronwy's other arm, Goronwy gave the power within him a little more leeway, and a warm bubble of air projected out from his center, enough to cover even Mabon. "Stay close to me."

None of them, even Mabon, whose sour expression was more firmly fixed on his face than ever, needed to be told twice. Yesterday, the wind and the cold wouldn't have affected him, but he was human today, and he hated the fact that he was reliant on a mortal—especially Goronwy—for his survival.

The snow grew thicker around them, but the ball of warmth floated through it untouched. They trudged along until they reached the rampart and the first gatehouse. As they pulled up before the twelve-foot high doors, the snow stopped.

Taliesin shook out his cloak. "The first test."

"That wasn't so bad," Goronwy said.

Taliesin shot him an amused look. "It could have been if you hadn't been here. And don't think there won't be more."

"What are we even doing here?" Catrin said.

Mabon craned his neck to look up at the gatehouse tower for signs of life. "My grandmother has not been collecting the Treasures. Why should she? She has no need of the power they bring. I'm not sure that they would even work for her." That was the most sensible speech Mabon had ever made. He seemed to know it too, because then he added, "Did my mother tell you to come here?"

"She did not. No," Taliesin said, "but I have come nonetheless."

He stepped back and raised his arms as if he was about to command the doors to open. Goronwy motioned that the others should retreat. Instead, Catrin darted forward and pulled on the door.

It opened easily—which seemed like a miracle until Goronwy saw the carnage behind it.

12

Cade

Penda was there to greet them as they entered the city, which was a dignity Cade hadn't expected. Still, the King of Gwynedd and his men were known for their martial prowess, and Penda *was* facing a determined Northumbrian army. He had to be thinking that it might pay to be respectful.

"You should evacuate the city," Cade said by way of a greeting. "Chester isn't defensible. Its walls are too long, and you have too few men, even with the addition of the twenty I've brought. If you leave now, Oswin will march into Chester, discover it empty, and march right back out."

"He will make it his seat!" Penda said.

They were standing in the former Roman *principia*, the headquarters building. It was built in stone and consisted of a large central courtyard, which was surrounded on the south, east, and west sides by a covered walkway fronting storage and sleeping rooms. On the north side of the cloister was the meeting hall with its central aisle and nave, resembling nothing less than a small church, though the Romans who'd built it hadn't yet been Christian.

"He won't, but even if he does, Oswin will find himself in the same position you are in: defending a too large city with too few men, facing a surrounding army with plenty of food and time."

"I have already sent the women and children to Westune," Penda admitted, "but my ancestors have held this city since the Romans left. I will not abandon it to Oswin of Northumbria!"

Cade scoffed. "Do not speak to me about ancestral lands. Your ancestors' right to this city comes from taking it from mine. No Saxon had yet reached Chester when the Romans abandoned us to *your* people."

Penda looked venomous, but he didn't argue. Perhaps he'd been telling himself about his rights for so long he'd started believing his own tales. "Nevertheless, Chester is defensible."

"How?" Cade said. "Northumbria has ladders and battering rams. They are coming over those walls; we will be forced to fight hand-to-hand before nightfall. You will lose everything and everyone to your pride."

"You can leave if you want to. I'm staying."

Cade narrowed his eyes at the Mercian king. "Just because my mother is your sister does not mean that I owe you my life. I came because you called, to discuss bringing my armies to fight alongside yours. I don't have an army today, and from what I've seen you barely do either. Why do you insist on fighting a battle you cannot win?"

Penda glowered at him, but when Cade didn't back down, he said, "I thought Peada told you why back at Dinas Bran."

Cade remembered—it was hardly as if he'd forget about the existence of a Treasure in Chester—but he wanted to hear it from Penda's own mouth. "Dinas Bran crumbled into ruin within hours of your leaving, so I am in no mood for evasions. Have you found the dish?"

Penda's jaw clenched, and he spoke through gritted teeth. "No."

"What makes you think you will find it before the Northumbrians come? Better to retreat and fight another day."

"We were hoping that you might be able to find it." Penda had the grace to look abashed.

Cade guffawed. "*That's* why you invited me here? To find the Treasure when you could not? Why do you think I would have any better luck in one hour than you've had in a lifetime?"

"You've collected many already," Penda said matter-of-factly. "Like calls to like. I know for a fact that Caledfwlch and Dyrnwyn alone could defend Chester."

"Two men cannot be everywhere at once, and Chester is a big city, as I said." Cade studied his uncle. Penda wasn't entirely wrong, at least about the Treasures being drawn to one another, and the sense of power that emanated from them. When Cade and his people had entered the city and then the great hall where Penda had his seat on the dais, the Saxons had cringed away. Cade had initially attributed their fear to him being Welsh, but now he wasn't so sure. Saxons were the least spiritual beings Cade had ever encountered, but even they could sense the way Cade's company was bristling with power.

Cade carried the mantle and his sword, Caledfwlch, on his person. Dafydd wore the sword, Dyrnwyn, belted at his waist. And Hywel kept the knife among his possessions. Since it was his family who'd protected it all these years, it seemed appropriate for him to be the one to decide when to use it. Not that it was any use against the Northumbrians, since it's purpose was to feed the multitude, as Christ had done, and the moment the blade had pierced Jesus's side, it became useless as a weapon. Taliesin had borrowed it during his recent journey and used it often.

At one time, Rhiann might have had the chess piece on her, since Mabon had given it to her, but she said it repulsed her, and thus had entrusted it to Taliesin.

Cade shook his head. "I will say this only once more: I am leaving, and I'm taking my people with me. This is a fool's fight, and one you can't win. If you choose to lose your life over a Treasure, that is your decision—and your delusion—not mine." He spun on his heel and headed back down the hall, the others following in his wake.

He had just put out a hand to open the doors, because the two men who guarded them weren't moving, when Penda called, "Wait!"

Cade stopped and looked back.

Penda was loping towards him. "All right, all right. You win. We will all go."

But then a bell tolled above their heads. Hearing it, Cade pushed open the doors, and everyone who'd been in the hall spilled into the courtyard. Cade crossed it to reach the main gateway to the street.

As he stepped out from the colonnade, Peada reined in amidst a small company of men. "They come! They come!"

"How many and how far?" Penda moved to hold the bridle of his son's horse.

"You can see their banners." Peada pointed north and then swung his arm to indicate the east as well. "Another quarter of an hour and they'll surround us completely."

Cade cursed and turned on Penda. "You and your pride will be the death of us all."

Penda firmed his chin. "I always meant to stand and fight."

"Are your men ready? Have you prepared oil and fire? Where are your archers?"

"I have them," Penda said defensively. "They're on the walls."

Cade narrowed his eyes as he looked at the Mercian king. To become an expert archer took long practice from childhood, and while all Welshmen high and low were so trained, most Saxons never valued archery enough to put in that kind of effort. If Penda was telling the truth, he deserved some credit for planning ahead. "We cannot win with the numbers we have now. You do realize this?"

"I am prepared to die for Mercia."

"Well, I am not." Cade spat out the last word.

"From what we saw earlier, they're predominantly on foot, my lord," Hywel said in Welsh in an undertone. "We should make use of the little time we do have."

Cade turned to Dafydd. "Take Angharad, all our horses, and whatever of Penda's strays who will go with you, and go now through the southern gate across the Dee to Caer Gwrlie. It is defensible, and your arm will keep it so."

"My lord, no! I will stand and fight with you!"

"If we wait any longer, it will be too late. It's already too late for the bulk of Penda's men." Cade gestured to Dafydd's sword. "That is enough to defend your retreat all by itself."

"What about you? How will you escape without horses?" Angharad said.

"We'll take the western tunnel," Cade said.

Dafydd subsided, nodding, but when Cade turned back to Penda, his brow was furrowed with puzzlement. "What tunnel?"

Cade studied his uncle, surprised that he didn't know. "The Romans built tunnels under every city and house in Wales—maybe throughout the whole empire. The tunnel from Chester runs from just inside the western wall under the river and to the watchtower on the other side."

"What watchtower?" Penda spread his hands wide. "We know of no such tunnel."

Bedwyr scoffed. "That would be because you were not born a Briton." He turned to Cade. "My grandfather was a man of Rheged, and one of the last to retreat from Chester before it was overrun by Mercia. He told me where the westward tunnel begins."

"Hopefully it hasn't collapsed due to neglect." Hywel shot a disgusted look at Penda.

"The Romans built it," Cade said by way of assurance. "While Dafydd leads the riders, we will get everyone else but a skeleton defense through the tunnel as quick as we can. Those who remain behind will make a show of resisting the Northumbrians, and then we ourselves will retreat." He looked to Rhiann. "I need you to go with Dafydd."

"You need me on the wall, as always."

She, as ever, had the power to stop Cade in his tracks just by looking at him. "Rhiann—"

Hywel stepped between them. "She's right, my lord. Penda says he has archers, but we have over a mile of wall to defend. He doesn't have that many. If the tunnel is passable, she can retreat with the rest of us."

"She carries my heir." Cade spoke through gritted teeth.

Rhiann moved closer. "I will not be used as your mother was—as a thing to barter to whomever the council chooses to replace you. We will live free or not at all. I'm staying with you."

Cade grimaced. "It will be just like Caer Fawr all over again."

"You needed me at Caer Fawr." Rhiann put the flat of her hand on his chest and looked up into his face. "That reminds me. I have thought up a name for our son: Geraint."

"*Cariad.*" Cade almost folded in on himself, and he found that he was unable to answer. Though, of course, he didn't have to.

"The archers will defend the north and east walls of the city." Penda spoke loudly in Saxon, interrupting their quiet conversation in Welsh. "I have thousands of arrows stockpiled."

Cade kept his eyes on his wife's face. "That's good, because it's likely we'll need them."

13

Catrin

As Taliesin had raised his arms, perhaps to call down some great power to burst the doors asunder—or at least to open them—Catrin had felt a whisper of the same power that she'd felt on the hill when they'd first arrived in the Otherworld. Then it had pulled her towards the castle, and even though they'd decided to come despite their fears, she'd attempted the whole time to block its call. She had every reason to distrust it, particularly after Goronwy had described the aura around the castle—and then the snowstorm. But still, the essence of the castle didn't feel malevolent to her.

And it seemed silly to not even try the doors before barraging them with magic.

As it turned out, when she pulled on the handle, the door opened easily on greased hinges. Her eyes went first towards the light coming from the middle of the courtyard where a fountain was adorned with trellises of beautiful flowers. A cascade of water spilled from it, and the breeze on her face warmed her from head to toe. Which made the sight of so many men on the ground all around the fountain and in the shadows in the gatehouse barbican all the more horrifying.

Goronwy pressed up behind her, gripping her upper arms, and then he moved her slightly aside so he could pass. He crouched next to the first body, which lay ten feet away, still within the barbican that protected the courtyard, and put two fingers to the man's neck. The man's face was gray with death and chiseled, almost as if it were made of stone, so when Goronwy looked back at Catrin and shook his head, she was not surprised.

Taliesin and Mabon moved quickly through the gateway, and at last Catrin followed. Although she remained focused on the dead men and bent to look into every face, Taliesin headed for the front doors to the keep that lay on the far side of the courtyard. Those great doors—nearly as large as the doors to the gatehouse—were closed too, and he pressed an ear to the wood to listen. At some point, Goronwy had unsheathed his sword, and he carried it point down. If the men who'd attacked the castle were still here, their small party was in real danger.

Catrin stood near the fountain with her hand to her throat. "Who could have done this?"

Nobody answered, least of all Taliesin. His silence may have been in large part because he knew and wouldn't say. Mabon straightened, having actually been feeling for a pulse in another man's neck, in imitation of Goronwy, and said, "Every one of these men looks nearly the same. Did you notice that, Taliesin?"

"That's because they're pawns."

"As we all are," Goronwy said.

"No." Taliesin shook his head. "I mean they are literally pawns. These are the animated forms of the chess set, one of the Treasures, placed here to guard the castle." He looked around. "This is all of them, it seems."

"What power!" A mixture of awe and greed crossed Mabon's face. That he wanted that power for himself went without saying, and Catrin knew in that moment that he would betray all of them without hesitation if it meant he could get closer to the one who wielded it.

Goronwy, however, had moved on to yet another body. "The guards were overwhelmed, either by skill or by numbers." He motioned with one hand. "Their killers weren't emotional—just systematic, killing one after another."

Catrin put aside the ache in her heart and approached Mabon, who had moved to the door to the keep to stand beside Taliesin. "How did you come by the chess piece you gave Rhiann? A king, wasn't it?"

Mabon looked mutinous for a moment, but then he laughed. "Why not tell you?" He gestured to the dead pawns. "It was a gift."

"From whom?"

Mabon waggled his finger at her. "That would be telling now, wouldn't it?" His expression turned thoughtful. "Perhaps he gave it to me because he had already planned this, knowing that he was going to destroy its magic."

A strange look crossed Taliesin's face, as if he didn't agree but decided at the last moment not to say so. Mabon wasn't paying attention anyway, having already pushed through the doors to the keep as if he was entering his own hall, rather than one full of ominous magic.

Catrin and Goronwy made to follow, but Taliesin stopped them, though his eyes remained on Mabon. "Don't believe him," he said in an undertone.

"It isn't destroyed?" Goronwy said.

"Whatever has happened here hasn't destroyed the chess set, only collected its magic into fewer pieces."

"How do you know?" Catrin said.

"I have the little king with me, and it still thrums with power."

Mabon, meanwhile, was halfway down the cavernous hall, and he waved a hand indicating they should catch up. "Hurry. I might be mortal, but I am not immune to what has happened here. There are more layers to this castle than what we see here."

Goronwy held back. "We should leave. We are hopelessly outmatched."

"There's no going back," Taliesin said flatly, and he gestured towards the gatehouse, "only forward."

Catrin spun around to look where Taliesin pointed. He was right. The gatehouse had disappeared, to be replaced by smooth stone. Even with Catrin's sight, she couldn't make out a seam in the wall. "I don't understand."

"Time and space don't move in the Otherworld the way they do in yours," Mabon said, again sounding more reasonable than Catrin had come to expect from the god. "That was the entrance. Now it isn't."

"Stay close," Taliesin said. "Mabon is right that no doorway leads to the same place twice, and I don't want to get separated."

The hall was built in white and gray marble, without colorful tapestries, a fire, or furniture of any kind. The only adornment lay in alcoves along the walls, containing silent gray statues with cold faces not unlike the dead pawns outside.

"Don't look at them." Taliesin strode forward after Mabon. "They don't like it."

Catrin hustled to keep up. "It's the rest of the chess set! What happened to them?"

"They are frozen by the same magic that animated the pawns. As the pawns were Dôn's guards, these are her servants." Taliesin pointed downward with one finger. "Note the way the stones of the floor emulate a chess board."

Now that Catrin knew what to look for, she could see the way the white stones alternated with a darker gray. She was more out of her depth than she'd ever been in her life.

"Quiet." Mabon put out a hand.

They'd reached the far end of the hall, where the only door was a narrow passage off to the right. The wind that whistled past them lifted a stray lock from Catrin's forehead.

Taliesin looked sharply at the *sidhe*. "What do you hear?"

"I don't know. Just ... something." Mabon's expression had turned wary, which was an unusual look for him. "The only way out is up. I'll go first." And without waiting for permission, he began to take the stairs two at a time.

"He's been here before," Goronwy said. "Let him lead."

"I'm wondering now if from the beginning this wasn't a trap for us," Catrin said. "Arianrhod could have given him to us knowing that Taliesin would take him right back into the Otherworld. Was that the plan from the start? Or did she not know what Taliesin intended?"

"Taliesin didn't know what he intended, exactly." The bard said, speaking of himself in the third person. Then he trotted up the stairs after Mabon, soon disappearing as the stairway curved around the central column.

Mabon's and Taliesin's long legs easily carried them up the steps. Catrin, however, was a much smaller person—and Goronwy much heavier—so very quickly the two of them fell behind. Catrin was breathing hard by the time they reached the top, having come up at least a hundred steps, which meant that the tower stretched far higher into the sky than she would have thought from looking at it from the outside.

Goronwy pushed open the door at the top of the steps, and they found themselves in a small, round room, perhaps fifteen feet across.

Catrin stopped on the threshold, stunned. "It's empty. Where are Mabon and Taliesin?"

"Don't come any closer." Taliesin's voice echoed around them. It held the tone of Command and stopped them in their tracks, but there was no sign of the bard himself.

"I knew I should have gone my own way." Mabon's voice faded into silence, and Catrin realized Taliesin had been speaking to him, not to her and Goronwy.

She looked wildly around. "What's happened? How can they not be here?"

"I don't know." Almost cat-like, Goronwy began to stalk about the small room. It was circular, and its only furniture was a table with a basin of water in it and a chest that when Goronwy lifted up the lid contained a bundle of rags wrapped around a length of old rope. Nothing else. The walls were plastered white and the floor was smooth wood, worn from feet treading on it for years beyond counting.

After making a complete circuit of the room, he returned to where she stood in the doorway. Out of fear that closing it all the way would lock them in as had the gatehouse doors, she hadn't allowed it to swing all the way closed.

Goronwy put his hand on the door at head height and eased it open. He looked down the dark stairwell and then stepped back to let the door close.

Catrin breathed a sigh of relief when it didn't seal. "There has to be more to this castle than what we've seen."

"As in, where Taliesin and Mabon have got to? Yes, indeed." Goronwy gave a derisive laugh, but she didn't sense that it was directed at her.

"We should go back down to the hall."

"I don't think so," Goronwy said. "There was no exit from there."

"Then how do we get out of here?"

"I think that's going to be up to you."

Now it was her turn to laugh. "What do you mean by that? I have none of Taliesin's power."

"But you have different power—and it's clear that you have power here. It was you who opened the door." He turned in a circle, taking in a full view of the room. "Have a look. Maybe you'll see things differently from me."

"I'm not a witch, no matter what people have said about me."

"You're a seeress. So *see*."

Catrin began to walk around the room as Goronwy had asked. She went first to the tiny window to look out. It faced west and showed her that they stood at least sixty feet above the ground, which remained snow covered, though the snow itself had stopped falling. The window was too small for either of them to fit through, and it led to a straight drop down, so it couldn't provide a way out. She moved on to the trunk.

Goronwy had left it open, and she stooped to remove the rags. Instead of disregarding them, as he had, she was of the opinion that nothing in this room was here by accident. She knelt, laid the bundle on the floor and, with careful movements, unwrapped it. The rope he'd dismissed as useless was revealed to be a horse's halter. As the halter was made of rope instead of leather, sliding knots replaced iron buckles to adjust the size to the horse.

Goronwy stood over her, his head bent and his fist to his lips. "I didn't even see it."

"You saw what you were predisposed to see. When Taliesin sang of a halter to tame any horse, you imagined rich leather adorned in gold and gems—" she gestured to the rope, "—not knotted hemp like a poor farmer might use to guide his broken-down carthorse."

Angry voices echoed up to them from the hall below, and then a man bellowed in rage. "Where did they go?"

"You fool! You scared them away!" The woman's voice was equally forceful—and equally angry.

The man shouted at her again. "I've been tricked! He told me I would find Treasures here!"

"You destroyed them!" The woman was fighting back, but if this was the man who'd killed the pawns, as it appeared it was, they needed to get out of there quickly.

Her hands shaking, Catrin hastily gathered up the rope and the rag wrapping and stuffed the bundle into her pack. Goronwy, meanwhile, strode to the door and looked out. "We need to get out of here, and not by the stairs, not without Taliesin or Cade to help us."

Catrin clenched her teeth to keep them from chattering. "Then how?"

"By *seeing* what nobody else can." He pointed to the small table. "What's that for?"

"It's a bowl with water in it." Catrin looked into it. At first glance, it appeared to be nothing more than a hand-washing bowl like any chamber might have, but then Catrin looked more closely at the etchings on the bottom and around the rim. They were hardly more than scratches, but she could still make out the spokes of a wheel and, within each set of spokes, was a rune from the old language. The bowl itself was made of bone, from what animal she didn't dare to guess. She looked over at Goronwy. "This isn't Dôn's. It's Arianrhod's."

"Can you make it work?"

Catrin laughed, though the sound came out more desperate than amused. "To what end? Scrying will not get us out of here—and besides, as I told you when we first met, I don't do magic. I just sense it."

"Like I don't do magic?" Goronwy looked down the stairwell one more time, then closed the door and dropped the bar across it. She had faint hope that a single piece of wood could stop a strong assault for long, but it made her feel better—safer that they were locked in. "We were separated from Taliesin and Mabon and brought to this room for a reason. That bowl is here for a reason. You may say you don't do magic, but it looks to me as if Arianrhod is telling you that you should." He lowered his voice. "I learned something new today. Maybe you are meant to too."

Catrin stared at him through several heartbeats, each one pounding loud in her ears, and then she nodded. Taking in a breath to center herself and calm her racing heart, she looked again into the bowl and touched the water with one finger.

Immediately, she was thrown into the midst of battle. Men screamed and died all around her, fighting hand-to-hand on a wall-walk. She was standing beside Rhiann on a battlement in the pouring rain, even as Rhiann shot arrow after arrow into a horde of oncoming Saxons. There were too many to count, and as Catrin caught her breath, a Saxon ladder hit the side of the wall on which Rhiann was standing. At first Catrin had thought she was at Caer Fawr, but then she realized she was somewhere else entirely.

Catrin jerked as an arrow shot by her head, and as she did so, she pulled out of the vision. The runes within the spokes of the wheel stood out as if they were etched in silver, and she spoke them out loud as she deciphered them: "Halter and stone, blood and bone. And in the center are the symbols meant to represent a man and a woman." Still breathing hard from what she'd seen, she bent her head, more shaken than she'd ever been in her life. "This isn't going to work."

Goronwy crossed the floor in two strides. "We have all those things! I am even a child of the blood as you are." More shouts came from below, muffled now by the closed door.

"It isn't that." She shut her eyes, not yet willing to speak to Goronwy of what she'd seen. She didn't know if the battle was happening right now, or if it was in the future. Either way, Rhiann's need was desperate—more desperate, in fact, than Catrin's own. "The stone we need is not ordinary. It's the Treasure, and Cade has it. If he were here—"

She broke off as Goronwy pulled the stone from his pack. It looked like nothing more or less than a typical river rock, unchanged from when the two of them had removed it from King Arthur's shield back on the road from Caerleon.

"How—"

"Cade gave it back to me, with the caution that Taliesin had insisted on it." Goronwy frowned. "Half the time Taliesin claims that his sight has failed him, and then he does this—"

"I am a woman, and I have the halter. You are a man, and you have the stone. The bowl is made of bone, and I have a bone knife that is sharp enough to draw blood."

"Surely a metal blade would cut more easily," Goronwy said.

Catrin grimaced. "Iron blocks magic. Bone is what is needed." She pulled the knife from a sheath at her waist and gave it to Goronwy.

He took it. "You're sure about this?"

"The only thing I'm sure about is that we have very little time."

14

Bedwyr

Bedwyr definitely could have been happier. He would have been a great deal happier if he had been on the walls beside Hywel, preparing to fight off the Northumbrian horde rather than down here in an underground room in the ruin of a building near the west gate.

Over two hundred years ago when the Romans had marched away from Britain, they'd left most of their cities as they'd been—stripped of all moveable goods, for certain—but intact. Whether building in stone or wood, they'd built to last, and they'd had no patience for anything that wouldn't stand the test of time. This building, however, which had to have been a guardhouse, since it was sitting over an escape tunnel, was either an exception to that rule or had been deliberately destroyed.

Bedwyr was guessing the latter. He'd never asked his grandfather if Rheged's army had destroyed the building on their way out, but it would make sense if they had. And yet, although two walls of the building had been knocked down, and the wooden roof was long gone, the room underneath the main floor was whole. Once they'd levered aside some of the larger stones, he'd been able to get to the trap door.

Above Bedwyr's head, the entire city was seething with activity. Penda was preparing both to defend the city and to leave it. Peada, however, had come with Bedwyr, along with a giant of a man whom Bedwyr had picked out of a line of soldiers as the most capable of moving large items.

Peada was counting out the beats. "Pull!"

Bedwyr and the Mercian soldier, Wystan, pulled up on their respective crowbars which they'd hooked around the double trap doors at their feet. Wystan was so strong that his iron bar actually bent a little, and at last the doors moved a little too.

"Rest," Peada said. "Are you sure there's a tunnel down there?"

Bedwyr was bent over with his hands on his knees, but he moved a hand to point to one of the torches that he'd slotted into a sconce on the wall. "The flame flickers."

Wystan nodded. "There's a stiff breeze blowing through the cracks. It has to be coming from somewhere.

Peada's eyes brightened. "Again."

Bedwyr and Wystan pulled on the doors but, after a count of ten, Bedwyr dropped his iron bar. "We're close, but I need you to find more men, preferably younger and stronger than I."

Peada was up instantly to do as Bedwyr asked, climbing the rubble-covered steps to street level. Here in the basement, the steady drizzle that had started to fall from the sky wasn't bothering them, but storms were as common in Britain in June as December, and it looked as if they were in for a big one. As far as Bedwyr was concerned, that wouldn't be a bad thing. Cade could fight outside during the day without his cloak only if the sun was hidden. Admittedly, rain was harmful to bowstrings, but it would make the ground mucky outside the city walls and the rungs of the Northumbrian ladders slippery. If the rain fell hard enough, it would also wash away blood.

"How did you know about this tunnel anyway?" Wystan eyes narrowed as he looked on Bedwyr with suspicion.

Bedwyr wiped at the sweat on his brow. "Before your lot came, my grandfather was one of the defenders of this city. When I was still in the cradle, he told me the story of following this tunnel out of the city as the walls were breached."

"He was a coward then."

Bedwyr scoffed. "He lived to fight another day, didn't he? He lived to father my father who fathered me, who is going to save your life and the life of your king—a man foolish enough to try to defend a city against overwhelming odds, just as the old King of Rheged did."

Wystan remained unforgiving. "I would rather die than surrender."

"Well—" Bedwyr grunted as he reached for the crowbar again, "—that's where you and I will have to differ, and it's also why your people will never conquer Wales. You would rather die heroically and stupidly than continue to serve your king." He shrugged. "I understand, but I can't respect that decision any more than you can respect mine."

Still looking fierce, Wystan picked up the crowbar, hooked it around the door latch, and with a great shout, heaved. The door flipped upward and fell open on the floor with a bang and a cloud of dust. Wystan himself staggered backwards now that he had nothing to pull against.

Bedwyr grinned. "That worked well, don't you think?"

Wystan glared at him. "You angered me on purpose."

"I did, and you very obligingly rose to the bait." Bedwyr bent to open the other half of the double-doors, revealing a stone staircase leading down. Bedwyr wrinkled his nose at the smell of mold and earth, but his sweaty face was cooled by the breeze, which brought fresh air into the room too. He heaved a sigh of relief that the tunnel was not only still open, but clear enough after all this time that the air wasn't poisonous.

Peada returned, but stopped on the threshold to the room with the men he'd brought bunching up behind him. "Is it safe?"

"I suppose it's time we found out." Bedwyr grabbed a torch and set off down the steps with it.

Peada didn't move, instead calling after Bedwyr, "It's a quarter-mile to the Dee."

Bedwyr didn't look back. "Then I'd better hurry, oughtn't I? The Northumbrians are coming, and you have men to gather. Why don't you do that while you wait for me to return." If they were going to flee the city, they needed to do it soon. "You coming, Wystan? Wouldn't want anyone to think you were a coward."

Wystan growled, and his heavy feet thudded on the stairs behind Bedwyr. "I don't like tunnels."

"If you fit, everyone will fit." Bedwyr reached a door at the bottom of the stairs. A simple lift of the metal latch opened it. Though dirt had accumulated against the bottom of the door, it wasn't so thick that one hard shove couldn't push through it.

"They'll be rats down here for sure." Wystan sounded like Goronwy.

Despite himself, Bedwyr was starting to like the Mercian. He shined the torch all around the stone ceiling and walls. The torch flickered in the wind, but the wick was fresh and well-oiled, so it stayed lit as he started forward down the tunnel. That the walls were still standing after all these years emboldened Bedwyr, and he picked up the pace. He could feel the pressure above him of the fight about to start, even though he couldn't see the soldiers on the walls. They needed a way out, and this was it.

A quarter-mile at a fast walk takes hardly any time at all, though to Bedwyr it felt like an hour before the path started rising up again, having dipped far down to run underneath the river. Sensibly, the Romans had lined with lead the part of the tunnel that ran under the river itself. Still, water dripped everywhere, and Bedwyr had a horrible feeling that the only thing that was keeping the river from flooding the tunnel was sheer belligerence on the part of those ancient builders.

"We're here." Wystan heaved a huge sigh of relief as he spied the exit: a ramshackle door that didn't want to open all the way. Somehow Wystan wedged his large bulk through it, however, and the two men came out the other side.

They found themselves in another cave-like basement, which was easily exited by following a flight of rough-cut stairs upwards. They came out at the foot of what had once been a guard tower, now so overgrown with shrubs and trees that it was no wonder the Saxon conquerors of Chester had never noticed it. The land to the west of the river was boggy—thus the long clay tunnel—and this was the first solid ground, which wasn't really all that solid. It was really raining now, and the earth under Bedwyr's feet was soft. It would take very little rain to turn the dirt to mud.

Bedwyr immediately looked to Wystan. "Run back to Peada and tell him that the tunnel is clear and to start getting people through it."

"What are you going to do?" Wystan said.

"Make sure no Northumbrians have come this far. They shouldn't know about the tunnel if your king didn't, but a company could have forded the river downstream to come at the city this way, precisely to stop anyone from leaving."

Wystan gave Bedwyr a jerky nod and re-entered the tunnel.

At his departure, Bedwyr took a breath and closed his eyes. He didn't have a hint of the *sight* or a touch of the *sidhe*, but he knew his grandfather's stories. One of them, as he'd related to Cade on the journey here, and the reason Cade had entrusted Bedwyr with the task of finding the tunnel, involved the sacred relic from Calvary that had been left behind at Chester. The priest in whose charge it had been placed had been killed at some point after he left the tunnel, along with a dozen men of Rheged, who'd died defending him. According to Penda, the Saxons hadn't retrieved the relic, however, and if they didn't have it, nobody had ever seen it again.

At the time, all Saxons had been pagan and without Penda's knowledge of Britain's Treasures. That meant there was a good chance the conquerors hadn't known what they had. In keeping with the Church's pledge of simplicity, the dish had been kept in a plain wooden box, and the dish itself was made of fired clay. If the dish had been destroyed, so be it, but as Bedwyr turned on one heel, surveying the land around him, he put together everything he knew about its disappearance, coupled with what he'd learned today about the Mercian occupation of Chester.

In short, they didn't know about the tunnel, which meant that the priest's company hadn't been ambushed right here. Otherwise, the Saxons, presumably, would have fortified this secret way into Chester, not left it to decay and become lost to time. How his grandfather had known the priests' fate was a question Bedwyr had never asked—for if all of the priest's defenders had died in the Treasure's defense, how had his grandfather learned the story?

Unless ... the witness had been Bedwyr's grandfather himself. The more Bedwyr considered the possibility, the more likely he found it. The story of Chester's lost Treasure wasn't one sung by any bard he knew. It was a story passed from grandfather to grandson on cold winter nights when only the family was present to listen. He knew too why his grandfather hadn't confessed that it was he who witnessed the ambush. That would mean that he'd seen the outcome but not fought, and he would have been ashamed.

Having himself fought in many battles by now, Bedwyr wished he could reassure his grandfather that he didn't blame him for hiding. Except for Wales itself, the Saxons had overrun all of the lands that had once belonged to the Britons. They were an onrushing tide that could not be stopped, and the death of a sixteen-year-old boy would have done nothing to avert Britain's fate.

Knowing that he had little time, since Peada would soon be leading men back through the tunnel, Bedwyr re-entered the basement with his torch and shone it all around the walls on either side of the door. Then he opened the door and went back into the tunnel itself.

He didn't know what he was looking for necessarily. Chances were, the Treasure, if it ever had been hidden here, was long gone. Chances were it had been destroyed in the ambush, not hidden before the priest ever left Chester in the hopes that he could one day return for it. But Bedwyr had to look.

He tried to place himself in the shoes of that long-dead priest, knowing what he held and fearing that it would fall into Saxon hands. The tunnel had been a well-maintained avenue connecting Chester with the guard tower on the other side of the Dee. If the priest hid the dish before leaving the tunnel, he would have chosen a place small enough to hide a box. As was the case with all but the lead-lined part of the tunnel, the walls and ceiling were exposed stone and well-mortared. Even after all these years and the weight pressing down from overhead, none of the stones had fallen.

Having set the torch in one of the many sconces the Romans had conveniently placed every twenty feet along the entire length of the tunnel, Bedwyr began running his hand up and down the walls all around the door and progressing away from it down the tunnel, growing ever more anxious that he wouldn't finish this task before either the Northumbrians—for whom he was supposed to be watching—or more importantly Peada and Penda—came. Then he realized he was making the usual mistake of a searcher: he was focusing on the area from his waist to his head, when a good hiding place was either in the ceiling itself or at ankle level.

He crouched to the ground and swept away the detritus that had built up close to the wall. The dirt and dust was several inches deep here, and soon he'd exposed a length of wall that hadn't seen air for nearly a century. Nothing seemed out of place or amiss, and he began to shift the dirt faster, frantically almost, fearing discovery at any moment.

And then, about three feet from the door, his hand hit an anomaly in one of the stones, which was otherwise a typical one-foot square block. Inset into the bottom right corner was a second square the width of his thumb. He prodded at it, and then he pressed it hard.

It sank half an inch into the wall, and the stone to the right popped open like a cupboard, revealing a hollow space behind the façade. A wooden box sat in the exact center of the cupboard, just as it had since the priest had put it there so many years ago.

Bedwyr was opposed generally to reliance on anything magical or from the world of the *sidhe*. The Treasures as a whole made him uncomfortable, and he much preferred to be grounded in what he could see, hear, and touch. But they were backed into a corner—and it wasn't as if his family hadn't protected the secret of the dish for three generations. He'd accepted the stories his grandfather had told him, as he'd accepted as his fate Cade's charge to find it.

With trembling hands, Bedwyr lifted the lid to reveal a plain ceramic dish, its burnish dark with age. The rim was cracked too, revealing the red clay from which it had been made and, impulsively, he traced his forefinger along the top edge. No earthquake shook the tunnel when he touched it, and the break felt smooth as butter beneath his finger. After a moment he took in a breath and pulled his hand away.

"This way!"

At the sound of Peada's voice, Bedwyr hesitated, but he knew that he didn't have enough time to pull out the box and hide it on his person and then put everything back the way it had been before they'd be upon him. He closed the lid, leaving the dish where it was, pushed the stone door shut, and then hastily swept the dirt back into place with long sweeps of his arm. Then he stomped all around the area before going to the exit and out the door into the basement.

He took the torch from the tunnel and put it into yet another sconce on the wall, this one inside the basement. By the time Peada appeared at the exit to the tunnel, Wystan at his heels and followed by a long line of men, Bedwyr was working vigorously at the front door to get it to open all the way. He turned to look as the Mercian prince appeared, grinned, and gestured him out the door.

15

Rhiann

Rhiann knew that Hywel missed having Bedwyr at his side, but she hoped that she and Cade could be a viable substitute. Cade wasn't as gruff or as amusing as Bedwyr, however. And he was currently invisible.

"They're going to wonder where you've gone," Hywel said out of the corner of his mouth. Rhiann, Cade, and Hywel were standing on the wall-walk near the city's northern gate.

"Peada is leading the men out of the city, so only Penda needs to know where I am, and I have chosen to make my stand away from him, as makes sense," Cade said. "He and I already talked about it."

"What if someone comes looking for you?" Rhiann said from Cade's other side. She held her unstrung bow loosely in her left hand, waiting for the Northumbrians to reach shooting range before stringing it. The rain was falling steadily and would ruin the bowstring if she strung it any sooner.

While Penda had made the wrong choice in deciding to defend his city, at least he hadn't been stupid about it: he'd placed painted stones on the ground at intervals outside the city walls to give the archers an idea of how far away their enemy was, so they could conserve their arrows until the Northumbrians came within range. Now that the sun had risen, Rhiann could see the markers in the distance.

"If someone comes for me, send them elsewhere, and if they say that they've just come from there, all you have to do is shrug." Cade clapped a hand on Hywel's shoulder. "If it even comes to that. We will all be killing Northumbrians, and who is going to have time to look for Gwynedd's wayward king?"

"You will be killing Northumbrians before they even touch me." Hywel rolled his eyes. "I won't take credit for what I have not done."

"We should be so lucky as to take credit for anything today," Rhiann said. "The Northumbrians are too many."

Under the mantle, Cade sighed. It was one of the miracles of its creation that by wearing it, everything about him, even his boots and sword when it was unsheathed, or his horse were he riding it, were hidden. He didn't even cast a shadow.

Rhiann frowned. "Why do Saxon women not fight beside their men? I've never understood it."

Hywel spoke through a tight jaw. "Because they have so many men, they don't need to call upon their women."

Rhiann's eyes remained focused on the oncoming force. "They do have a lot of men." It was intentionally the kind of flat tone Bedwyr would have used, and Hywel smiled, as Rhiann had hoped he would.

"It's almost time to start shooting, Rhiann," Cade said.

"How exactly did we get here?" she said. "Yesterday we were at Dinas Bran talking about baby names."

"We're through! We're through!"

They all spun around to look down at the messenger, a young Mercian man with a shock of blond hair, flattened now by the rain. He could see only Hywel and Rhiann on the wall-walk, so in Cade's supposed absence Hywel was the one to ask, "What do you mean *we're through?*" He glanced back over the walls. "The Northumbrians have breached the wall?"

Rhiann put out a hand to him. "No. He means Bedwyr found the tunnel's exit."

"We are evacuating the city now." The messenger nodded at Rhiann. "King Penda asks that you stay on the wall while he speaks to Oswin. If he can stall, we can get everyone out but the last few before the Northumbrians attack."

"That means you need the archers to stay the longest," Rhiann said.

The messenger bowed. "Indeed, madam." He straightened. "King Penda requested that I find King Cadwaladr and ask him to join him. Do you know where he is?"

"I can't tell you at present," Hywel said, and though that wasn't entirely a lie, Rhiann was glad that he'd taken it upon himself to deceive, rather than leaving it to her. "But I'll get the message to him."

"Thank you." And the messenger ran off.

Both Rhiann and Hywel looked at Cade, though to an outsider it appeared that they were looking at each other.

"I'll go down to the gatehouse," Cade said.

"But—" Rhiann started to protest.

"It's raining harder than ever, and I'll wear my regular cloak and helmet. Nobody will wonder at that because it's raining. I'll be fine." Rhiann saw the ladder shift, indicating that Cade had started down it, but then it stopped moving, and all of a sudden, she found herself swept into his arms. They kissed, and then she moved back a few inches so she could smile up at him. She was invisible to everyone else, but since she was touching him, she could see him.

Hywel looked around. "Uh ... my lord?"

Cade laughed. "Stand on the far edge of the wall-walk, so it looks as if Rhiann was behind you all this time."

Hywel did as he was bid, and Rhiann bumped into his back. He turned around. "Does it feel any different?"

She laughed. "No, which is why it's so strange."

Hywel laughed too. "I wouldn't say that's the only reason."

They looked down towards the gatehouse in time to see Cade step out of the guardroom at its base as if he'd been inside it the whole time. Penda was just coming from the hall. They'd sent all the horses away with Dafydd and Angharad, so he was on foot, which might appear somewhat odd to Oswin when Penda walked instead of rode from the gatehouse, but it was unlikely that it would be something he'd remark upon. He wanted the city. How he got it wouldn't matter to him.

Rhiann then turned to look at the oncoming Northumbrians. They'd stopped just beyond the first markers as if they knew they were there—which perhaps they did. Saxons weren't archers as a rule, but they'd been fighting the Britons long enough to account for their presence among an enemy's ranks and maybe even employ a few of their own as Penda had.

The same messenger who'd come to speak to them before appeared below once again, this time with a white flag on a long pole. He tossed it up to Hywel, who caught it, and then the man climbed the ladder to reach the wall-walk.

"Thanks," he said breathlessly, and then ran to a second ladder that would take him to the top of the gatehouse tower. He began waving the flag back and forth above his head.

The Northumbrians couldn't miss it, but no commander stepped forward from Oswin's line. Rhiann approached the edge of the battlement, her brow furrowing. Refusing to acknowledge a white flag wasn't unprecedented, but it was rare and deeply concerning. And then a horn sounded from within the Northumbrian ranks, followed by the roar of two thousand voices.

Oswin wasn't going to talk. The Northumbrians were charging.

16

Catrin

Catrin began to chant words in the old language that she dredged up from somewhere deep inside her, words that she almost didn't know the meaning of until she spoke them:

> *An ancient watchman*
> *Stands on the castle walls*
> *Blood turns to bone and then stone*
> *The wind whistles in the passages*
> *The Cymry are abandoned*
> *And evil shows itself at last.*

Catrin cut the fat part of her left hand and matched it to the cut Goronwy had already made in his. They clasped hands as their blood joined and dripped into the bowl.

"Why evil?" Goronwy asked.

"Shh!"

Boots pounded on the stairs, and Catrin counted them lucky to have made it this long without being caught. She gripped Goronwy's hand tightly, even as he turned to look at the door. But it was as if a veil were shimmering between them and it. The door burst open at the behest of an enormous, wild-haired man with an axe blade bigger than Catrin's head. Then the room wavered one more time—and vanished.

They both staggered, and Goronwy reached for the post that appeared at his left shoulder. Their right hands were still joined, and Catrin stumbled towards him and thumped into his chest.

He held her close. "It's all right."

"You can't know that."

"It feels like it to me."

Goronwy touched his forehead to hers—just a quick movement, such that she almost wasn't sure he'd done it until she looked up at him.

He smiled.

Goronwy didn't smile often, except at jests he himself might tell, but in this moment his smile lit his whole being, and it was as if he had a halo of joy around him. "I wouldn't have forgone this journey for all the silver in the treasury."

Catrin looked away, but she couldn't keep her own smile from her lips. "Is that so?" She glanced around to examine where they found themselves. The tower room was gone, to be replaced by a common stable. To distract herself from thinking about Goronwy, she said, "Is this where Taliesin went?"

"I don't know, but I don't think so." All of a sudden, something in his tone changed, and the glow that had surrounded him disappeared, to be replaced by a sudden darkness. "Taliesin will be fine."

Her brow furrowed in puzzlement. "I know, Goronwy. If anyone can take care of himself, it's Taliesin."

Goronwy nodded, as if she'd answered a question for him. "I don't want to see you hurt, Catrin."

"Why would I be hurt?"

"Does he know how you feel?"

"Does who know how I feel? About what?" She felt a rising impatience. They were running from gods, and he was talking in riddles.

Goronwy sighed. "Do I have to say it out loud?"

"Apparently you do, because I have no idea what you're talking about." She peered around the corner of the stall, but it was so dark in the stable, she couldn't see beyond a few feet. Time didn't pass normally in the Otherworld, as

Taliesin was always telling them, and she had no idea if hours had passed since they'd arrived at Caer Wydr or only heartbeats.

"Taliesin. Does he know that you're in love with him?"

Catrin froze, and she was glad that the darkness in the stall in which they found themselves prevented Goronwy from seeing her clearly because she knew she'd flushed red to the roots of her hair. Then she straightened, telling herself not to be a coward, and looked directly into his face. "I am not in love with Taliesin."

"You do remember that I can see auras, right?" Goronwy's voice was gentle. "Even in the dark, yours tells me that you are in love."

Catrin took in a breath and, before she could change her mind, said. "Not long after the battle at Caer Fawr, Taliesin told me, in that casual way of his that makes it seem like he feels nothing, that he had seen a future—one future out of a hundred other possible futures—in which I walked beside him. But once followed, that path led to darkness and despair, and he would not take it nor allow me to think it possible."

She canted her head, revealing what was in her heart in a way she had told herself she never would again. "I'm not a fool or a girl just barely into womanhood to love where love isn't wanted. I'm not one to cry into my pillow at love unrequited. Taliesin meant what he said, and for months I've had no hope in that direction—nor have I wanted any."

Though she'd managed to be straightforward until this moment, now she evaded Goronwy's eyes. She'd spoken the truth, but not all of it. To have the little attention she'd paid to Taliesin deflected had set her back a pace for a while. It had been a long time since she'd cared enough about any man to let her feelings show. It had been a long time, living in the woods alone as she'd been before Goronwy came to her, since she'd had any friends at all.

"I admit that I thought I was in love with him, but he isn't like you and me. Did you know that, inside, he's a hundred generations old?"

"I suppose I did." Goronwy stood still as a stone.

"While he needs love and human companionship, lest he become something other than a man, he can *see* in a way no other man in this world sees." She faced Goronwy, able again to look into his eyes without embarrassment. "I cannot imagine living that way, knowing everyone's secrets, dreams, and desires—not because he can read minds but because he can see future outcomes and paths followed." She supposed if Taliesin had been interested in her in the way she'd been interested in him, those long spells of detachment might have eventually driven her mad. Of course, they'd been part of his attraction in the first place.

"You are beautiful, wise, and kind," Goronwy said. "You have a tender heart, and for that reason alone, Taliesin should be sorry to have walked away from you. I suspect part of him is sorry too."

"It wasn't meant to be." Catrin lifted one shoulder. "It truly is no matter."

"But—" Goronwy frowned, and she could tell he was looking at her still with his inner eye. She hadn't known that his ability to see auras could expose the truth in her so profoundly. She should have known it perhaps, since she could see auras too sometimes, but apparently not like he did.

She sighed. "Goronwy, I am in love, but not with him."

Catrin took in a breath, on the verge of saying more, but she caught herself before she did. The companionship she'd gained from living at Dinas Bran had changed her life. She had come on this journey in part to take care of Taliesin, who needed taking care of—if nothing else was true, that was—and in part to figure out where she was going to go from here. Looking at Goronwy now, she accepted for herself, even if she never spoke the words out loud, that a woman didn't always have to wander far afield. The best answer could be right in front of her.

She saw the moment that understanding hit him too.

He cleared his throat. "You're—you're in love with … me?"

She smiled sadly. "I would never have said anything, since I know you don't feel the same way. But you had to see auras—" She shook her head, gazing up at him, wanting what she could never have. And then she threw caution to the winds. They were in the Otherworld, in peril, with no way back and no notion of what lay ahead. It was a time for taking risks. She gripped the fabric of his cloak as it lay on his chest, stood on her tiptoes, and pressed her lips to his.

Though he kissed her back, he didn't put his arms around her. Feeling like a fool, she let go and backed off from him, intending to pretend the kiss had never happened.

But before she'd gone two steps, Goronwy caught her hand. "Actually—" He pulled her back to him, and this time his arms came around her fully.

The kiss was slow and sweet, and by the end Catrin was trembling in his arms.

Goronwy smiled down at her. "You can see auras like I can. You should have known that I'm in love too."

"Well, well. I was wondering when one of you would make it here. I confess, you are not what I expected."

They both spun around at the voice, Goronwy still with his arms around Catrin. A man stood fifteen feet away near one of the stalls, carefully brushing out the mane of a coal-black horse Catrin could have sworn hadn't been there a moment before. Beyond him sat a golden chariot that shimmered and glowed, almost as if it was giving off its own light rather than reflecting the light of the man's lantern.

Goronwy's hand went to the hilt of his sword, and the man put out a hand in appeasement. "Now, now. No need for that." He was broad-chested, built like the most imposing blacksmith Catrin had ever seen. His size alone made a mockery of his soothing words. He wore gold war bands around his biceps, a long cloak that trailed the ground, and black, knee-high boots, polished until they shone like a mirror. Though Catrin didn't know exactly who this was, he was no man.

Goronwy recognized it too. He swallowed hard and bent his head. "I apologize for disturbing you, oh great one."

"No need for that either, especially when you bring me such lovely company." The god-man dropped his brush onto a nearby shelf and approached.

Catrin was still holding Goronwy's hand. Instead of dropping it in her nervousness, as she might have done yesterday, she clenched it tighter. At least their hands had stopped bleeding. As children of the sight, both had been well aware of the power of blood even before they'd used it just now, and she didn't want to leave any more of themselves lying around this fantastical palace than they already had.

"My lord." Goronwy bowed. "I beg your forgiveness for infringing on your place, and ask if you would honor me with your name."

The god grunted. "So you are educated in the important things." He pointed a finger at himself. "I am Manawydan." He indicated the doorway behind them. "Few have the ability to escape the guards."

"Do you mean the chess pieces?" Goronwy said.

"Of course."

"We weren't running from them," Catrin said. "They were dead before we arrived."

Manawydan's eyes narrowed. "Just because they're immobile doesn't mean they're dead."

"You misunderstand, my lord," Catrin said as tactfully as she could. "Their bodies lay scattered about the castle's courtyard."

Manawydan's staggeringly handsome face froze into position for a moment, not unlike one of the chess pieces. However, he absorbed that news without further comment. "But you found the doorway to here." He had a tendency to make statements that could have been questions if his inflection had been different.

"If by doorway you mean Catrin used the scrying bowl," Goronwy said, "then yes. Otherwise, the room at the top of the tower was a dead end."

Manawydan cocked his head. "You think so?"

Catrin looked at Goronwy. "He's right. Taliesin and Mabon got out."

"They don't count," Goronwy said in an undertone.

Manawydan's attention had become fixed on Catrin's face. "Mabon is here?" He took a step towards them, and for the first time his tone was menacing.

"Taliesin brought him, at Arianrhod's request!" Goronwy pulled Catrin a few steps away from Manawydan, towards the chariot. Without having to talk to one another, they both knew what it was, knew they wanted it, but didn't know a way to take it without either inspiring the wrath of Manawydan or outright stealing it. In truth, they needed to take both the horse and the chariot, and they couldn't do that without Manawydan's permission.

"Manawydan! Cousin! I must speak with you." The voice came from outside the stable and was that of the man in the hall who'd shouted at the woman—and presumably had followed them from the room at the top of the tower.

Manawydan growled under his breath. "What is Hafgan up to?"

"Perhaps he is helping Mabon in his search for the Treasures of Britain?" Catrin said.

If Manawydan expression had been menacing before, now it was downright terrifying, but this time his ire wasn't directed at Goronwy and Catrin. "It was my grandfather's intent to pull Mabon's teeth, not spur him to greater insurrection." He paused. "Unless—" Without finishing the thought, he started walking towards the exit. "Coming, Hafgan!"

"My lord, unless what?" Goronwy put out a hand. "Please tell us. We are on a quest for the Treasures ourselves, but not because we want to use them. Cadwaladr ap Cadwallon, my liege lord, seeks to keep them safe."

Manawydan hesitated. "I have heard of this Cadwaladr. He has made an impression even here, for he was made by Arianrhod, and his doings have entwined with Mabon's."

Catrin curtseyed deeply. "Please, sir. We are mortals caught up in events beyond our understanding, but we seek only to serve."

His lips pursed, Manawydan waved his hand. Between one heartbeat and the next, the stable and everything inside and out became encased in a thick mist. Then he grabbed Goronwy's arm, and to Catrin it looked as if lightning had struck the knight. The god's grip was like a vice, and Goronwy could neither move nor speak. Manawydan leaned in and spoke in Goronwy's ear, words that Catrin couldn't hear. Then he pulled back and said in a hoarse voice. "I will speak to my grandfather about what has passed this day. Take the horse and the chariot and go! Stop him."

"We will try," Goronwy said, and then he staggered as Manawydan released him. A moment later, the god had disappeared out the door.

Catrin was shaking from head to foot, but she pulled the halter from her pack and ran towards the horse. "What did he say to you?"

Goronwy had recovered enough to move to the chariot, grab the tracers, and haul it towards her. It was made of gold but was lighter than any mortal-made vehicle and moved with barely a whisper.

He set the yoke around the horse. "Just the name: Efnysien."

"Manawydan's half-brother?" Catrin gaped at him, horrified. "May the gods preserve us."

"Why? Who are these people?" Goronwy looked contrite. "I endeavored to forget everything my mother taught me."

"Manawydan is the son of Llyr, Lord of the Sea, and the grandson of Beli. Efnysien is his half-brother, and he makes every jealous and malicious younger brother—human or *sidhe*—appear benign by comparison." Catrin felt a grimness settle on her shoulders. The glow of warmth of Goronwy's attentions was long gone. "We need to go now!"

"How? Where?" Goronwy took the reins in one hand and helped Catrin into the chariot with the other.

"Just speak the place where you want to be or the name of the one you want to be with and the chariot will take you there." Catrin gripped the bar in front of her as if they were already riding the winds.

Goronwy didn't ask how Catrin knew that, which was a good thing since she wasn't sure where the knowledge had come from. Only that she was right.

He clicked his tongue at the horse and said simply: "Cade."

17

Rhiann

Rhiann had been in this situation before, and she wasn't any happier about it than she'd been the last time they'd faced unreasonable odds and had no choice but to stand and fight. Side-by-side with Hywel, she was loosing arrows into the mass of Northumbrians running towards them, though most of the arrows stuck harmlessly in the shields that the Northumbrians held in front of them.

They had no help from Penda's men either. Between when the Northumbrians started towards them and now, all the rest of the archers had disappeared from the walls. In fact, a quick glance around showed Rhiann that the two of them were alone on the northern wall. They had intended to hold off Oswin's men to give Penda's army a chance to retreat, but Cade had never intended that the only ones left defending Chester were Welsh.

"It's time to go, Rhiann." Cade appeared between them, as if out of thin air. "I've ordered the rest of our men to the tunnel."

Rhiann snorted her disgust in a very unqueenly fashion. "And leave you two to face death alone? I already agreed that I wouldn't. Besides—" in between arrows, she jerked her head to indicate the street behind them, "—it's too late."

Hywel growled in his best imitation of Bedwyr. "Thanks, Penda, for your help."

Cade swore, uncharacteristically loud and long. The city was lost before they'd begun to defend it. Northumbrians were already coming over the eastern wall. A horde of them raced for the inside of the gatehouse tunnel, prepared to open the gates to the army crossing the field to the north.

Rhiann returned her gaze to the men coming towards them. They had few bowmen, so she wasn't worried about her exposure on the wall, but the situation was hopeless.

Then Cade swooped out his arms like a falcon in flight. In a moment, all three of them were sheltering beneath his enveloping mantle. "Move!" He held on to their arms and hustled them west along the wall-walk. Chester's walls had been constructed such that a guardhouse lay every fifty yards along them, and the companions ran through two without stopping until they reached the northwestern, more isolated section of the city. In order to descend a ladder to the street, Rhiann and Hywel had to leave the protective covering of the cloak and become visible again, but once they were on the ground, Cade gathered them to him again.

"How are we going to escape this madness?" Hywel said.

"We'll find a way—" Cade broke off as a company of twenty Saxons came loping down the street towards them. The small company included both Northumbrians and Mercians.

"What is going on?" Rhiann breathed out the words.

Hywel gaped at the soldiers. "In the name of—" he broke off, seemingly thinking better of invoking whatever god or saint had been in his mind. If they'd learned anything in the months with Cade, it was to be careful of calling upon the *sidhe*.

The Saxon leader had his hand above his head, emphasizing with finger pointing how he wanted the company to separate.

"They're searching house-to-house," Hywel said. "Are they looking for the dish?"

Cade's laugh was heavy with irony. "No. They're looking for me."

Rhiann bent her head, an ache forming in her belly. "Penda's invitation to Chester was a trap all along,"

"It was." Now that the truth was out, Cade was matter-of-fact. He dragged them both around the corner of a street and across it to a ladder propped against the western wall of the city. "Quick—up to the wall-walk again before they see us."

Hywel came out from underneath the cloak first, followed by Rhiann. Cade sprang up the ladder at her heels and reached the top only a moment after she did. A heartbeat later, they were all touching Cade again and invisible to the searching soldiers on the street.

They still needed a way out, however, sooner rather than later. Rhiann went to the nearest crenel and looked down through it. The wall was twenty feet above the ground, which was too far for Rhiann or Hywel to jump, though Cade had easily made jumps of similar height.

"They'll give up looking eventually. We can simply wait until they're drunk tonight," Hywel said, "and leave by an unattended gate."

Cade's expression was fierce. "We would live, but our men would be dead by the time we escaped. They've gone through the tunnel with Peada. They may be fierce, but they're too few and cannot withstand a hundred or more."

At Cade's frank assessment, the ache in Rhiann's stomach worsened, and she felt tears pricking the corners of her eyes. She'd grown used to Cade's ability to get them out of any situation, no matter how dire.

Then a crack of lightning split the night, and Rhiann reeled at the burst of energy expelled from it. Not even a heartbeat later, a golden chariot pulled by a coal-black horse rocketed through a rent in the sky and came to a halt in front of them, hovering thirty feet in the air, just outside Chester's wall.

Goronwy grinned from the driver's platform. "Seriously, do I have to do everything myself?"

The three companions gaped at him, and then Catrin leaned backwards from where she'd been hidden from their view by Goronwy's bulk. "Hurry, get on! We have no idea how this thing really works!"

"How were you able even to see us?" Hywel climbed into the crenel in front of him, leapt across the six feet of space between the wall and the chariot, and landed with a thump on the back behind Goronwy.

Catrin caught his arm. "I'm guessing that it's because the mantle is a Treasure, and so is the chariot." Then she waved to Cade and Rhiann that they should jump too.

Cade held Rhiann's waist in a tight grip, and they jumped together, landing hard on the platform, such that the chariot shuddered. It held, however, and Goronwy glanced back. "I'm not even going to ask what you were doing at Chester, so I'll just ask where we should go now?"

"Bedwyr is at the western entrance to a tunnel that runs from the city, under the Dee, to an abandoned guard tower on the other side," Cade said. "Penda lured me into a trap, and I'm afraid that Bedwyr has been caught in it even more than I."

"Worse?" Goronwy laughed, and instead of mockery, his voice was full of joy—and a touch of glee. "Then I suppose we'd better hurry."

18

Bedwyr

Bedwyr had long since begun to regret every moment of this day. Cade's men had been interspersed among Peada's as they'd traveled through the tunnel, but as each had appeared in the doorway, with a few terse words he'd directed them away from the exit and towards the right side of the small clearing, near the trees that grew beside the river.

While the Welsh were grossly outnumbered— once Dafydd and Angharad rode away, they'd been left with fewer than twenty men—Bedwyr wanted them to situate themselves in some kind of defensible formation. He'd never trusted Penda or Peada, and this moment didn't seem to be a good time to start. More importantly, his warrior's instincts told him that something wasn't right about what was happening here—neither the numbers of Saxons coming through the tunnel nor the way they seemed to be in less of a hurry than they should have been. They were relaxed, as if they didn't have an army of Oswin's men breathing down their necks.

Then Penda himself appeared, not last as he'd promised, and not with Cade and Bedwyr's other companions.

And he wasn't taking no for an answer.

"Put down your weapons!" The King of Mercia wore a superior smile, and his eyes gleamed. Bedwyr's men had their backs to the river. While some could swim, most could not, and Bedwyr wouldn't leave any men behind. Fortunately, Penda's lack of bowmen meant that if he was going to fight Bedwyr and his men, it was going to be sword on sword, so Penda was going to lose men in the process too.

Bedwyr gripped his sword tighter in his fist. His palms were sweaty, but he'd roughed up the leather grip so it didn't slip in his hand. "No." He could no more surrender to Penda than he could sprout wings and fly. He prayed that his wife would forgive him for dying so soon into their marriage—and that Hywel would forgive him for not seeing the danger sooner.

"We're with you, Bedwyr." The voice came softly from behind him—it was one of the younger men in Cade's company, though since he'd lived through the battle at Caer Fawr, he was far older than his years.

Bedwyr crouched, his sword in his right hand and a knife in his left. He was sorry now that he hadn't kept the dish with him. It was said to grant the bearer every wish—a double-edged blade for certain, and one to be used only at the last end of need. But that's what this had become.

So instead of praying for deliverance, he did what every good soldier would do in his position: he endeavored to stall. "So this was a trap all along? You never meant to ally with King Cadwaladr?"

"Oswin gave me one chance to avert the assault: give him my nephew." Penda scoffed. "I couldn't believe my luck when I saw his banner this morning. He walked right into my hands."

"But he had said he wasn't coming." Bedwyr was genuinely confused. "With Oswin on your doorstep, what was your plan?"

Penda shrugged. "Capturing Cade had been a long shot from the start. Without him, nothing changed, and I was forced to mount a defense."

"But then you did have Cade, and Oswin still attacked."

From over to the right, Peada sneered at Bedwyr. "That was for show, for your king's benefit."

"How did you let Oswin know that Cade was here?"

"As soon as you entered the city, I rode out to tell him." Peada spoke as if nothing could be more obvious. Bedwyr recalled that Peada hadn't been in the hall when they'd arrived, and it had been he who brought the news of Oswin's imminent attack.

"You lost men!" Bedwyr was irate. "So did he!"

"I lost many fewer than I would have." Penda said. "Last chance."

Bedwyr was opening his mouth to deny Penda again when Hywel's voice came low in his ear, speaking from underneath the mantle, since nobody else seemed to know he was there. "I always knew Penda was a snake, but I'm hurt that you almost started this feast without me."

Bedwyr blinked and tried not let his surprise and relief show on his face. His eyes still fixed on Penda, he muttered out of the side of his mouth in Welsh. "Took you long enough. I found the Treasure."

"Is it safe?"

"Yes, for now. I say we leave it where it is. Meanwhile, I'm hoping you have a plan."

"Oh, yes." Hywel gave a low laugh. "Cade is the plan."

Then, as if responding to Hywel's words, though he couldn't have heard them at that distance, Cade strode out of the woods to the west. Sword unsheathed, he cut a path through Penda's men without even bloodying its tip. Such was the power emanating from him that the Mercians fell back whether or not they wanted to. Peada stood his ground the longest, but even he retreated from Cade's contained might.

Hywel remained an invisible presence at Bedwyr shoulder, ready to fight if needed, though Bedwyr was feeling much more cheerful all of a sudden about whether or not fighting would be necessary.

Cade halted five paces in front of Bedwyr, facing Penda. "My men and I are leaving now."

Penda sneered. "How? You are outnumbered."

Cade raised his sword such that it pointed upwards, kissed the hilt, and then dropped the tip so it pointed straight at Penda. "You said yourself that Caledfwlch and Dyrnwyn alone could hold Chester. While you see here only Caledfwlch, are you ready to put the issue to a test?"

Earlier, Penda's face had been full of glee, but now he glowered at Cade, though he still didn't give way. Then a flaming arrow landed a foot in front of him, causing him to step back involuntarily. The arrow blazed between him and Cade, despite the rain that continued to fall. Bedwyr looked upwards to his left to see Rhiann perched on the top of the mound upon which the guard tower had once stood.

Behind him, the rest of Cade's men shifted into ready stances for fighting. They were an elite force, better trained than most of Penda's men and seasoned by the battles they'd fought at Cade's side. They'd lost friends at Caer Fawr, and to a man they would not go down now without taking many Mercians with them.

Penda knew it, but he was still warring with himself. His men grossly outnumbered Cade's, and he longed for the kind of power Cade wielded just by existing. In that moment, Bedwyr experienced an uncomfortable flash of prescience, which told him that Penda had, in fact, dreamed of power, which was how Mabon had seduced him before Caer Fawr. Penda had hoped to take Caledfwlch and the mantle for himself—along with whatever other Treasures he could salvage from the fallen bodies of Cade's men. But he truly didn't want to put Caledfwlch or Cade to the test. Penda had seen the weapon in action at Caer Fawr, and time and distance had not dimmed the memory.

"Go, Penda," Cade said with far more magnanimity than Bedwyr was currently able to muster. "Live in peace for the few months you have left."

For a heartbeat, Penda's face showed no expression. Then, before the fire in his eyes could return, Goronwy came out from behind a tree a few paces from Peada, hooked his arm around Peada's neck, and drew him back against him with a knife to his throat. "I'm tired of your games, Penda. When you and your men have disappeared into the tunnel, I'll let your son go and not before."

"Coward!" Penda spat on the ground, though he didn't move from where he stood.

Goronwy laughed, not at all offended. "Did you miss the part about the Welsh being pragmatists? Besides, I'm not the one who betrayed the High King of the Britons. Cadwaladr's name will live on forever, while your name will fade into nothingness within days of your demise. You have sealed your fate. Go."

Bedwyr wasn't the only one gaping at Goronwy, who never gave speeches. His old friend seemed to glow with a hint of the power Cade himself wielded. And though Goronwy's words angered Penda, in the end the Mercian king had no choice but to comply. He motioned jerkily with one hand, and his men retreated behind him into the basement that would take them to the tunnel's entrance.

Cade watched them go, and then gestured Goronwy forward, still with Peada as his prisoner. When they reached him, Cade tipped his head to let Goronwy know that he could release Peada. Goronwy obeyed and stepped away.

Penda was beyond words and simply shook his fist at Cade, but Peada said, "This isn't over, cousin."

"It is, Peada. You just don't know it yet," Cade said.

The moment the two Mercians disappeared into the basement, Cade turned to his men, "Go! Go! Follow Hywel."

Hywel whipped off the cloak, tossing it to Cade as he went by him and heading for the woods. As one, the Welsh company followed. Even as Cade bundled the fabric under his arm, he walked backwards after them while at the same time making a hurrying motion with his hand. Rhiann bounded down from the mound, fleet as ever despite her pregnancy. Goronwy waited until she reached where he was standing and then jogged beside her, leaving Bedwyr and Cade to bring up the rear.

They were several dozen strides into the woods, heading south, before Bedwyr spoke. "They will pursue us, don't you think?"

"Wouldn't you?" Cade said. "Penda is a gravely disappointed man. I hate to think what bargain he struck with Oswin such that he let him into Chester unchallenged."

"He was going to lose anyway. To him, it was worth the risk to acquire a Treasure or two. With them, he could have taken it back. Who would there be to stand in his way once you—and all of us—were dead?"

"What I want to know," Rhiann said breathlessly as she leapt over a fallen branch, "is if Taliesin foresaw this, and if so, why didn't he say anything?"

"Taliesin wasn't seeing very clearly when last I saw him," Goronwy said.

"Speaking of the bard, where is he?" Bedwyr said.

"He didn't return with Catrin and me. It's a long story," Goronwy said.

Then the thunder of horses' hooves reached them. At first Bedwyr thought it was Penda bringing reinforcements. Then when this proved not to be the case, he assumed it was Taliesin's doing, which would have been the real answer to his question to Goronwy. But a moment later, as they came out onto a road, he realized he was wrong on all counts. It was Dafydd, riding at the head of a company of men. He had brought their horses and was accompanied by a golden chariot which rolled so smoothly along the road it didn't even seem to be touching the ground. It was pulled by a black horse and driven by Catrin.

The chariot settled to a stop in front of Goronwy, who casually stepped onto the platform beside Catrin and took the reins from her.

Along with a kiss.

"Apparently, I missed more than one story." Bedwyr halted near Cade, who threw himself upon one of the horses Dafydd had brought and pulled Rhiann up behind him. He looked up at Cade. "Where is Taliesin, really?"

"I don't know exactly," Cade said. "I do know that our next task is to find him."

* * * * *

In the quiet of Caer Gwrlie's hall that evening, Bedwyr lay on his too-soft pallet and gazed up at the ceiling, unable to sleep. They'd left the dish in its stone cupboard just inside the tunnel, rather than sending Bedwyr back in the cloak to retrieve it. Cade had looked at him curiously when Bedwyr had insisted that it was too risky to return to Chester so soon right under Penda's nose. But because he'd been adamant, Cade had given way.

In the darkness of the hall, Bedwyr raised his hands before his eyes. They were trembling. He had longed for a way for himself and his men to survive the confrontation with Penda, and almost as he'd wished it, Cade had come from nowhere and rescued them. Maybe, if Bedwyr were to ask Taliesin about it, Cade would always have been there to rescue them.

But maybe not.

Was it Fate? Or was it the Hand of God, reaching down and touching him because he'd touched the dish?

He clenched his hands into fists to steady them, understanding for the first time what it might be like to be touched by the *sidhe*. Then he sighed and rolled over, his eyes on the fire crackling in the middle of the hall. He consoled himself with the knowledge that they'd acquired three more Treasures, at least in a manner of speaking, and none of his companions had died. It wasn't the ending any of them had hoped for, but it was a kind of ending, and one of which Bedwyr thought his grandfather could be proud.

Acknowledgments

I have many people to thank, not only for their assistance with *The Last Pendragon Saga*, but who have helped make my books better and my life sane for the last ten years.

First and foremost, thank you to my family: my husband Dan, who told me to give it five years and see if I still loved writing. Ten years on, I still do. Thank you for your infinite patience with having a writer as a wife. To my four children, Brynne, Carew, Gareth, and Taran, who have been nothing but encouraging, despite the fact that their mother spends half her life in medieval Wales. Thank you to my parents, for passing along their love of history.

Thanks to my beautiful writing partner, Anna Elliott, who has made this journey with me from nearly the beginning. Thank you to the many support groups to which I belong (you know who you are).

And thank you to my readers. You make it all worthwhile.

About the Author

With two historian parents, Sarah couldn't help but develop an interest in the past. She went on to get more than enough education herself (in anthropology) and began writing fiction when the stories in her head overflowed and demanded she let them out. While her ancestry is Welsh, she only visited Wales for the first time while in college. She has been in love with the country, language, and people ever since. She even convinced her husband to give all four of their children Welsh names.

She makes her home in Oregon.

Printed in Poland
by Amazon Fulfillment
Poland Sp. z o.o., Wrocław